To: Sebastian

Never Stop R

MW00896200

What About Dylan?

Enjoy Dylan's journey!

R. Jetleb

R Jetleb

CAVERN
OF DREAMS
PUBLISHING

Ordering Information:
Books may be ordered through Cavern of Dreams Publishing
71 Mohawk Street
Brantford, ON N3S 2W5
1-226-802-3954
(Discounts available for volume orders)

-

Published by
CAVERN OF DREAMS PUBLISHING
Brantford, Ontario, Canada

Library and Archives Canada Cataloguing in Publication

Jetleb, Regina, author
       What about Dylan? / written by Regina Jetleb; edited by Bethany Jamieson-Mansour.

Issued in print and electronic formats.
ISBN 978-1-927899-76-2 (softcover).–ISBN 978-1-927899-77-9 (PDF)

       I. Jamieson-Mansour, Bethany, editor II. Title.

PS8619.E853W42 2017   C813'.6   C2017-902176-1
                                                    C2017-902177-X

ACKNOWLEDGEMENTS AND THANKS

I would like to once again acknowledge my fantastic editor,
Bethany, at Cavern of Dreams.
I trust her implicitly with my work—I don't trust easily, but
having seen the consistently high quality of her editing, I
never have any doubts after sending off my work.
Thanks, Bethany!

A debt of gratitude to Mary, the driving force behind
Cavern. I am so fortunate to have met her. I have found not
only a wonderful publisher, but a friend. An author friend!
Someone with whom I can discuss our mutual passion for
excellent, high quality, well-edited writing,
and also share confidences, laughs,
and advice on things we have in common.

I appreciate the work done by Jen in designing/creating a
beautiful cover, and bringing my Dylan to life.
I extend my thanks, once again, to Terry Davis from Ball
Media in producing an eye-catching, appealing cover.

Last, but not least, a heartfelt thanks to
my husband, Matthias,
for his careful reading of my manuscript, and helpfully (and
in the nicest possible way) pointing out all my
inconsistencies, and advising on how to keep the events in
my story as realistic as possible.

Dedication

For my beautiful niece, **Hannah**, who kept me (who was in high school a good three decades ago) current and informed on the ins and outs of what it is like to be a grade nine student in 2016.

For my niece, **Eva,** who has a smile that lights up a room. She eagerly provided several very useful suggestions for the direction of the story.

For my irrepressibly bright nephew, **Adam**, who shares my insatiable thirst for reading as many books as he can get his hands on. He, together with his sister, Eva, helped me solve many sticky plot points with their ingenious, and clever suggestions.

Finally, for my four-year-old niece, **Sylvia**, who was the inspiration behind many of the mannerisms and behaviours of my youngest character.

AND FOR ETHAN:

An avid, enthusiastic reader,

and future author himself.

He suggested a sequel to

What about Hailey?

that focused on her younger brother,
Dylan.

Thanks to Ethan,

Dylan now has his own story to tell!

CHAPTER ONE

Dylan Williams-Marcotte quickly scooped up the folded scrap of paper that landed on his desk while his grade four teacher, Mrs. Cane, had her back turned to the class, writing on the whiteboard. He risked a quick glance beside him at his best friend, Ethan, who had tossed the note, and grinned.

Ethan gave him a thumb's up. As Dylan started stealthily unfolding the note to read it, he heard someone clear their throat behind him. Dylan glanced over his shoulder. Mrs. Peters, the classroom assistant, was standing at his desk. Busted! He had forgotten she was nearby, organizing the art supplies in the back of the room.

"Now what do we have here?" she asked, taking the note out of Dylan's hand.

Dylan smirked. He was so glad he and Ethan had worked together on writing notes in code. All Mrs. Peters would see on the paper would be groups of numbers. Only Dylan and Ethan had the key to deciphering the code and reading the message. Ethan's message to Dylan would remain private.

"What is the meaning of this?" Mrs. Peters tapped the paper, her normally soft voice growing louder. Mrs. Cane turned from the blackboard and was facing her class. The room was silent as nineteen pairs of ears tuned into Mrs. Peters and Dylan.

Dylan felt himself turning red. He tried to slide down in his seat and make himself smaller. He wished Mrs. Peters would leave him alone. Her official title was 'Education Assistant' and she was supposed to be there for the whole class, but she had been in all of Dylan's classes since grade one. He knew she was really there to help him learn, and in case he had a seizure.

Stupid seizures! Why did he have to be the only kid around who had seizures when he got a sudden high fever? Back when he was very little, in grade one, he used to describe his seizures to anyone who asked as "falling down and having the shakes." Now he understood what was happening to him during a seizure. His mom, a nurse, had come to school on Career Day when he was in grade two and had shown the class a video and talked to them about seizures. She had explained that the brain is sending electrical signals to the muscles in the body to tell it what to do. During a seizure, too many brain cells are sending signals at the same time and it causes an overload. A person may pass out and shake all over. During a seizure, the person cannot control what their body is doing.

When Georgia, a very friendly, talkative girl in his class, said she still didn't understand, his mother explained it another way: "It's sort of like when you're watching TV and the picture gets blocky or freezes completely for a minute and then goes back on properly again."

"Dylan, I'm disappointed in you," scolded Mrs. Peters, breaking into his thoughts. "This is the third time this week you've been caught with notes when you should be listening. I'll be giving your parents a call later today to let them know about your poor behaviour."

Uh oh! Dylan didn't like getting in trouble. It made his stomach ache. He needed to say something quickly so Mrs. Peters wouldn't be so mad at him. "Sorry I wasn't listening in class," Dylan mumbled, looking up into Mrs. Peters warm, brown eyes. "I won't do it again. Please don't tell my parents."

Mrs. Peters knelt so she was eye to eye with Dylan. She smiled sympathetically. "Sorry, buddy, your parents deserve to know about all your behaviour, good and bad."

Dylan slid down even further in his seat and shrugged his shoulders as Mrs. Peters patted him on the back and returned to the back of the class to resume tidying the craft area.

For the rest of the morning, Dylan found it hard to concentrate on the spelling words and math questions Mrs. Cane was talking about. Dylan hoped his parents weren't going to be too angry with him for reading notes when he should have been paying attention in class. His parents were always talking about how education was so important, and how the more he knew, the further he would go in life. His sister, Hailey, was in grade nine in high school, and she had been grounded for an entire weekend for cheating on a test. Now they were going to get more bad news about Dylan not listening in class! He hoped they wouldn't ground him this weekend and not let him go to Ethan's for a sleepover!

At lunch, Dylan picked at his ham-and-cheese sandwich. His stomach still hurt and now so did his head. He hoped he wasn't going to get a fever.

"Hey, Dyl," said Ethan, gesturing at Dylan's unfinished sandwich. "You eating that?"

"Nah, I don't feel hungry," replied Dylan as he took a sip of his water.

"Your parents are probably just going to give you a lecture," suggested Ethan as he picked up Dylan's sandwich and took a bite.

Dylan was happy to have a best friend like Ethan. They understood each other so well. Dylan didn't have to explain to Ethan how worried he was about getting caught with the note, Ethan already knew. They had been friends since Dylan had moved into the house next to Ethan's way back in grade one.

That had been one of the happiest days of his life, the day he and his sister moved in with David and Alexandra Marcotte, who would adopt them permanently into their lives a few months later. Dylan had only been two when his biological parents died in a car crash and he didn't remember them much, except for the framed photo of them he liked to look at whenever he was in Hailey's room. David and Alexandra were the best parents ever, and while he knew they would always love him, he didn't want them to be disappointed in him. He wanted them to be proud of him. On days like this, he felt as if he didn't measure up at all.

That afternoon, Mrs. Cane handed back a math test on long division the class had written on Monday. Dylan's heart thumped quickly as he sat at his desk, waiting for his name to be called to get his test back. It had been a hard test, and even though Mrs. Peters had spent extra time with him at lunch and nutrition break on the day before the test, carrying and remainders were still confusing for him. Also, Dylan wanted to be a detective and solve mysteries when he grew up, and he was sure he wouldn't need to know such complicated math. Codes were much more fun than math. Even though some codes used numbers, it was easy if you had the key. Dylan and Ethan had worked for one whole afternoon making a code where A equalled 1, B equalled 2, C equalled 3, and so on. All you had to do was match up the letter in the word with the number. No math needed.

Mrs. Cane interrupted Dylan's thoughts. "Dylan, come up to my desk for a minute, please."

Dylan approached Mrs. Cane's desk slowly, fingers crossed behind his back. *I hope I passed, I hoped I passed...* he chanted quietly to himself.

"You'll have to retake the test," said Mrs. Cane as she handed Dylan his paper. "You just need a little more time with Mrs. Peters working on lining up the numbers and with carrying," she explained. "Have your parents sign the top of the test beside your grade and my note about retaking it, and bring it back tomorrow."

Dylan nodded. He didn't dare look down at the grade; he knew it wouldn't be good. Today was turning out to be an awful day. Dylan trudged back to his desk slowly. The rest of the afternoon dragged.

It wasn't until he and Ethan were packing up their bags at the end of the day that he looked at his math test. Uh oh. 10 questions right out of 30. A fail.

"Don't worry," Ethan tried to reassure him on their walk home, after Dylan had showed him the failing mark, "You get to take the test again. You'll just have to study harder with Mrs. Peters. You'll get it pretty soon for sure. You're smart. You came up with our super secret code." Ethan paused a moment before continuing to speak. "Uh, sorry about throwing you notes. It's my fault you keep getting in trouble."

"It's okay, I was too slow hiding the note so I wouldn't get caught." Dylan kicked a stone along the sidewalk. "I just hope Mom and Dad still let me sleep over at your house tomorrow. They're gonna be mad I wasn't listening in class *and* I failed a test."

Ethan shrugged. "You can always sleep over next week if they're really upset. It's not a huge deal, Dylan," Ethan reassured his friend.

Dylan and Ethan spent the rest of the walk home taking turns kicking a pine cone back and forth between them.

"Bye, Dylan," said Ethan once they reached Ethan's driveway. "I'll be waiting at my window at eight o'clock if you want to tell me if you're in trouble or not."

Dylan gave Ethan a quick thumb's up and turned away from his best friend to start toward his house. He didn't think he would be in the mood to use their special flashlight code tonight. It was a simple code he and Ethan had thought up a year ago and had been having great fun with ever since. A one second pulse of the flashlight meant *yes*, and two pulses of light meant *no*. Three pulses meant *call me*.

Dylan took a deep breath, crossed his fingers and toes, and trudged up the walkway to his front door, worrying the whole way. How much trouble would he be in and how disappointed would his parents be?

CHAPTER TWO

"Hi, Dad," Dylan called after letting himself in and tossing his backpack on the floor beside Hailey's sneakers. Her school let out a few minutes before his and she always got home five minutes before he did.

"Hey, Little Man," answered his dad as he got up from where he was sitting at the kitchen table typing to give Dylan a hug. "How was school?"

"Okay," mumbled Dylan, pressing a hand to his stomach. It felt like a bunch of bees were buzzing around inside his tummy.

"Just okay?" asked his dad, running a hand through his short, dark hair and glancing at his laptop on the table.

"Yeah," answered Dylan. His dad didn't seem to be annoyed with him and he wondered if his teacher had called home like she said she would. Maybe the awful buzzy feeling in his tummy would go away if he knew if he was going to be in trouble or not. He took a deep breath and blurted, "Did my teacher call you?"

"Oh, yeah, she did ... Lucas, no!" shouted his dad, hurrying over to his laptop. Lucas had stopped colouring and had pulled the computer toward himself and was smashing down keys randomly.

Dylan watched as his dad pried Lucas away from

his laptop and positioned himself opposite his youngest son, making sure he had eye contact with him. "No. Daddy's work. Don't touch," he carefully signed.

Lucas was almost four years old and hard of hearing. Dylan's parents had adopted him three months ago, in the summer. He had come to live with them in February, three weeks after his third birthday. Lucas had a hearing aid in one ear and a cochlear implant in the other ear. Dylan's mom had explained that the special device had been surgically implanted and it could do the work of the damaged parts of Lucas' inner ear by providing sound signals to Lucas' brain.

Dylan thought he knew what Lucas wanted as he watched his dad try unsuccessfully to head off a temper tantrum. Lucas wasn't looking at David and he was signing wildly, his vocalizations becoming louder and louder. Dylan went over to the laptop and quickly clicked on YouTube. Once there, he typed in Thomas Train and up popped several videos featuring Lucas's favourite character.

"He wants to watch Thomas videos, Dad," explained Dylan. "He keeps signing the 'T' for Thomas and then the word 'train.'"

"Thanks, Dyl," sighed David, sinking into a chair. "Lucas is signing too quickly for me to figure it out fast enough. I'll have to remember that one." David ruffled Lucas' short blond hair. The newest addition to the family had calmed down quickly and was engrossed in the video. "I guess I'll have to finish my chapter later."

Dylan forced a smile. "No problem." He wished he could feel as useful and important as he had last spring when he and his family were taking sign language classes at the community centre. Sign language was easy for Dylan; he thought of it as just another code. Although his dad was an author and great with writing words, he seemed to have a lot of difficulty learning the signs for the words. Dylan's dad had relied on him a lot to review the lessons with him after each class.

"Oh, shoot!" exclaimed David as he glanced at the clock in the kitchen. "Mom is going to be home any minute and I haven't even started dinner." He opened the fridge and peered in.

"Now which leftovers am I looking for?" he mumbled to himself as Hailey came into the kitchen from her room.

"I'm starving," she declared. "What are we having?"

"Good question," replied David, glancing over at Hailey in the doorway. "Do you remember what Mom said this morning before she left?"

Hailey huffed impatiently and ran her finger along the purple stripe on her black leggings. "She left a note on the counter, Dad."

Hailey grinned over at Dylan and then at Lucas.

10

R. Jetleb

"Hey, Thing One," she said to Dylan. "Looks like Thomas the Train saved Thing Two, staring at the screen over there, from throwing another fit."

Dylan threw his sister a quick grin and picked up his backpack to head to his room. At first, he had thought it was cute that Hailey called him and Lucas 'Thing One' and 'Thing Two' after that Dr. Seuss movie, but now it made him feel small and like a nuisance.

Dylan dropped his school bag on the floor of his room and flopped across the bed on his back. He wasn't quite ready to tell Hailey to stop calling him Thing One. He was glad she paid any attention to him at all. Now that she had started high school, she spent a lot of time in her room, on her phone, or doing homework, or figuring out which outfit she was going to wear, or how she was going to style her shoulder-length, wavy, light brown hair. It had only been six weeks since the start of school but it felt more like six months to Dylan. They used to spend a lot of time together and now she didn't seem to have as much time for him. He missed hanging out with her.

Dylan sighed, rolled over on to his stomach and pulled his backpack onto his bed. He unzipped the bag and slowly pulled out the math test. Now he'd have to wait until after dinner to show it to his parents.

Dylan lay on his bed a long time, daydreaming. Daydreaming was his favourite thing to do and it always helped him to feel calm. He liked to imagine he was a detective with the Toronto police force and he was the one everyone went to for help in solving crimes.

Dylan was just imagining getting an award for 'best detective' when Hailey yelled "Supper!" from the kitchen. Dylan got off the bed, folded up his math test, and put it in his jeans' back pocket. He rinsed his hands quickly in the washroom and headed into the kitchen.

His mom had come home from her job at the nearby hospital. "Hi, Mom," Dylan greeted her with a huge smile and hug. Hugging his mom at the end of a day was the best feeling in the world and always made him happy, no matter how badly he was feeling. Imagining winning that award had helped Dylan feel calmer, and now with his mom's hug, the jumpy feeling in his tummy had disappeared completely.

His mom squeezed him back, ruffling his shaggy, brown hair. "Good day at school, Dylan?" she asked as she pushed Lucas' chair closer to the table and poured milk into his plastic Thomas cup.

"There's a Halloween dance at school, Mom," said Hailey as Dylan took his place at the table, glad for once to have Hailey interrupt him. It hadn't been a good day at school and Dylan wanted to wait a bit before showing his parents the test. "Can I go?"

"I assume it's going to be chaperoned by teachers?" replied Alexandra.

Hailey rolled her eyes. "Obviously."

"There's no need to roll your eyes and take that tone, Hailey," admonished Alexandra. "It's a perfectly reasonable question."

Dylan took a small bite of his burger. Leftover burgers didn't taste as good as the ones right off the grill. He took the top bun off the burger, squirted out a generous dollop of ketchup and then added mustard. He replaced the bun and wondered when would be a good time to show his parents the test. He wished Hailey didn't have such a knack for annoying Alexandra. Hailey had a temper that matched her mother's and sparks flew between the two of them regularly. Showing the test to his mom when she was aggravated with Hailey wasn't a good idea.

"Shame about the Wongs," said his dad. "Jerome was saying it was a priceless family heirloom."

"What happened at the Wongs?" asked Dylan.

Dylan noticed his parents exchanging a quick glance before answering. He knew that glance was code for something, but what? What were his parents communicating to one another that they didn't want him to know?

"It's nothing, the Wongs lost a treasured set of solid silver cutlery."

"How do you 'lose' a whole set of cutlery?" Hailey was snorting when Lucas pushed his plate on to the floor with a crash.

"Lucas!" said Alexandra, getting out of her chair. "We don't drop supper on the floor. We're cleaning this up now," she signed and said. Lucas threw himself out of his chair, picked up the burger he had dropped, and started tearing it apart and throwing pieces around the kitchen.

"Lucas!' shouted David. He slid out of his spot at the table and hurried to Alexandra's side to help calm Lucas, who was now sprawled on the floor, kicking and flailing.

It took several minutes to settle Lucas down and make sense of his signing. "You forgot to break up his burger in bite-size pieces," said Hailey as Alexandra began cutting up a new burger for Lucas.

"Oh, right," moaned David, slapping his forehead in frustration. Lucas did much better at the table and ate more if his food was arranged in small segments on his plate.

Dylan speared some peas with his fork and groaned quietly. This dinner was going from bad to worse. Most nights, suppertime went smoothly. It figured, on the night he had bad news, that dinner had turned into a circus. Dylan worried there wouldn't be a good time to show his parents his failing math test.

By the time they were all eating fruit salad for dessert, however, Dylan was feeling better. Hailey had apologized for her attitude, and Alexandra and David had given her permission to go to the dance. Lucas had contentedly eaten his supper, one bite-size chunk at a time.

"Your turn to rinse the dishes and load the dishwasher," Hailey reminded Dylan after supper. "I've got a ton of homework." Hailey headed out of the kitchen to her room. Dylan took the test out of his pocket and smoothed it out. It was now or never.

Alexandra was finishing her milk and keeping an eye on Lucas, who was still eating his fruit salad.

David was writing notes on the notepad he always had at the table to capture ideas for his book so he wouldn't forget, and looked up when Alexandra leaned over and tapped the notebook. "You'll want to jot down we need a new padlock for the side door on the garage," she said. "The old one won't lock."

"Right," answered David, tearing a fresh page off the pad. "I'll start a shopping list."

"Um, I have a test to show you," began Dylan tentatively as he placed the paper in front of his mom.

Alexandra picked it up, read it, and frowned. "This is disappointing. I thought you had extra study time with Mrs. Peters before that test?" She didn't wait for Dylan to answer. "Pass me your pen for a second, David," she said, moving Lucas' bowl away from the edge of the table where it was in danger of being elbowed off by her youngest son.

Alexandra quickly signed the test and handed the pen back to David. "Your dad said your teacher called.

15

You've been caught passing notes..." At that moment, Lucas spilled his milk all over himself, and Alexandra jumped up to clean up the mess.

"You need to pay attention in class, not pass notes," Alexandra said, mopping up milk from the table and the floor. "That poor test is proof of that." She helped Lucas off the chair and turned to her husband. "David, would you run the bath for Lucas, please?"

"Sure," answered David, heading out of the kitchen.

"Time for your bath," signed Alexandra to Lucas, wiping his ketchup smeared face with a damp cloth.

"Any more calls from your teacher and you're grounded," she added from over her shoulder as she and Lucas left the kitchen.

Dylan stood alone in the quiet kitchen, thinking. It didn't seem like he was in too much trouble, although his mom did say she was disappointed in him. He wasn't sure how much his dad had heard, he had been so involved in writing his notes. At least he wasn't grounded. Not yet, anyway.

Dylan quickly rinsed the dishes, loaded them into the dishwasher and turned it on before heading to his room. On the way past Hailey's room, he glanced in. She was at her desk, on her phone, frowning at a textbook in front of her. "Why do we have to solve for x anyway? This is math with numbers, *not* letters," she grumbled.

In his room, Dylan got out his spelling and started work on it. He was glad he only had spelling homework and not that complicated math stuff Hailey was working on.

In bed that night, Dylan tossed and turned. The house was quiet, but Dylan's mind wasn't. Dylan was glad he was not in as much trouble as he thought, but he was feeling left out. He was stuck right in the middle of Hailey and Lucas, and his parents seemed to pay a lot of attention to his older sister and his younger brother. It felt like nobody had time for him anymore. Then a horrible thought crossed his mind: what if Mom and Dad decide to adopt even *more* children? They wouldn't have any time left for him at all then!

Dylan threw his covers off and sat up, heart pounding. Suddenly, he remembered rule number five of the house rules posted on the fridge. *Talk it out if it bothers you so much that you can't sleep at night.* Why hadn't he thought of it before? He just needed to talk about his worries with his parents and everything would be fine again.

Dylan hurried out of his room. His dad was in the living room, typing furiously on the laptop. He looked so busy Dylan didn't want to disturb him.

When he didn't find Alexandra in the kitchen, he peeked into Lucas' room. Sometimes his mom stayed in Lucas' room until he fell asleep. Not there. He headed for Hailey's room next. Her door was closed. He pressed his ear to the door and listened hard. Their words were muffled, but he thought he heard his mom saying something about boys and dancing and appropriate behaviour. It sounded like they were having a serious, important talk.

Dylan slowly backed away from the door and returned to his room. He crawled in under the covers and blinked away tears. His dad was busy writing his novel. His mom was busy looking after Lucas and having important discussions with his sister. Hailey was busy adjusting to life in high school. There just wasn't any time for Dylan. What did he need to do to get noticed? Everyone else in his family got paid attention to, but what about Dylan?

CHAPTER THREE

"This is going to be great," said Ethan, draping his bed sheet over his desk chair and dropping a heavy dictionary on the chair to keep the sheet secured in place. "Good thing you weren't grounded. Building forts is not as much fun when you're by yourself," he continued.

Dylan knelt to tuck one edge of the sheet more firmly under the books on Ethan's bookcase. "Yeah, I guess."

"You don't sound too happy," observed Ethan, brushing his wavy red hair out of his eyes.

It was Friday, and Dylan was spending the night at Ethan's. The boys had spent all of lunch planning out everything they wanted to do on this sleepover. Number one on the list was to make a fort, fill it with blankets and pillows, and spend the night in it. They would even have their pizza supper and snacks there! It would also be dark under the sheets, and they could work on adding to their flashlight code and make goofy shadows. It was supposed to be a lot of fun, but Dylan was having a hard time feeling excited about their planned activities.

The best thing about having a best friend was that he knew you so well, you couldn't hide anything from him. That was also the worst thing about having a best friend.

Ethan enjoyed reading and was really good with words, especially when it came to describing his feelings. Dylan was still sorting through his thoughts about feeling left out at home. This morning during nutrition break at school, he'd only been able to say he wasn't in the mood when Ethan asked him why he didn't use their flashlight code last night.

Dylan shrugged, and changed the subject. "Let's put our pillows and sleeping bags in."

"Yeah, and get our flashlights too," Ethan replied, crawling out of their fort.

They were smoothing out their sleeping bags when Ethan's mom knocked on the open door to Ethan's room. "Hey, guys, I've got the stuff ready to make your mini pizzas."

"Cool," answered Ethan. "We'll be right there."

Ethan's mom knelt and peeked into the fort. "You've got your EpiPen handy, right?"

"Uh, I know where it is," Ethan offered cautiously.

"Ethan Michael Nicholson! Knowing where it is and having it beside you, ready to use, are two very different things! Does Dylan know where it is? Because once you start having an allergic reaction, your throat will close up and you won't be able to speak to direct Dylan, or me, for that matter, to where your life-saving medication is!" Ethan's mom was red in the face, and her eyes shone with unshed tears. "Go and get it now, please!"

Ethan slid free of the fort quickly and hurried from the room.

"Sorry, Dylan, for raising my voice," apologized Mrs. Nicholson. "It's just, it's such a serious allergy he has..." Her voice trailed off, and she rubbed at her eyes.

Dylan rolled his flashlight back and forth under his hand. Ethan was allergic to nuts, and if he even smelled them, he would react immediately. His face, lips, and eyes would swell up, along with the breathing tubes in his throat. Ethan wouldn't be able to breathe, and his heart rate would get very fast and become very weak. The EpiPen Ethan always carried with him contained a chemical called *epinephrine,* which would stimulate his heart to beat strongly, and relax muscles in his airways and lungs so he could breathe more freely. It was a sudden, life-saving burst of energy.

The gross thing, for Dylan, was knowing the medicine had to be injected, and the needle was long enough to go through jeans or a snowsuit. Ethan's mom had shown him the EpiPen back in grade one, and they'd watched a short video about it. Dylan remembered being relieved you never actually saw the needle because it was kept in a protective plastic casing. Ethan's EpiPen came in a special tube, and once you took the cap off the tube, you just needed to plunge the red end of the tube against your thigh and hold it there for ten seconds. After that, 911 had to be called and Ethan needed to go to the hospital for follow-up treatment.

Dylan had only seen Ethan have an allergic reaction once, back in grade two, and it had been scary to see his best friend so sick. But he had also seen how fast an EpiPen could be used and how quickly it worked.

"It's okay," said Dylan softly. "I understand."

"Right, of course you do. You're Ethan's best friend. I know your mom worries about you too." Dylan knew Ethan's mom was thinking about Dylan's seizures.

"It was still in my backpack," said Ethan, returning with his EpiPen. "Sorry, Mom," he said quietly. "I'll make sure I always have it on me," he continued, reassuring his mother.

"That's good, Ethan," smiled Mrs. Nicholson. She clapped her hands. "Let's get into the kitchen and start on those pizzas."

It was fun grating cheese, slicing pepperoni, and spreading sauce on the English muffins that would become the mini pizzas, and by the time the pizzas were baked and eaten, Dylan was feeling much happier.

"We can help with the cleanup, Mom," volunteered Ethan after the last crumb had been picked off their plates.

"No, I'm good, you guys go have fun in your fort."

"Thanks, Mom," replied Ethan, giving her a hug.

"Wow, your mom was really upset about your EpiPen," said Dylan once they had manoeuvred themselves into the tent and made themselves comfortable. "I thought she was going to start to cry for a second."

Ethan gave a long sigh. "Yeah, she's more worried than usual 'cause of what's been happening at the park."

Dylan scrunched his face in confusion. "What's been happening at the park?"

Ethan sat up from his lounging position. "Oh wow, wait 'til you hear this. Yesterday, or maybe the day before, some creep—or creeps—smeared peanut butter all over the railings on the stairs going up the climber with the three slides, and all along the edge of the curly slide!"

Dylan could hardly believe his ears. "Who would do something that awful when they know there are people out there with serious allergies to peanuts! That's totally..." Dylan broke off, unable to find a word that came close to describing how despicable that act of vandalism was.

"No wonder your mom's so upset," continued Dylan.

"Yeah, and remember a few weeks ago, how we

found all that broken glass spread all over the bouncy bridge on the climber and we had to go home?" said Ethan.

Dylan nodded, and the boys sat in somber silence, thinking about the events at their favourite park.

Ethan broke the silence after a few minutes. "I don't want to think about jerks ruining kids' fun at the park anymore. How about we have some flashlight wars?"

Dylan grinned. "I like that idea."

"Okay, then," smiled Ethan. He reached for his flashlight. "Battery check," he announced solemnly.

"Starting battery check," intoned Dylan as seriously as he could while trying not to giggle. He carefully unscrewed the battery compartment of the flashlight, dumped out the battery, reinserted it, and screwed the cover on tightly.

Ethan was doing the same thing with his flashlight, and once his check was complete, he began the countdown. "3, 2, 1. Final. Battery. Check." At the end of his pronouncement, the race was on to be the first to shine their flashlight in the other boy's face.

"A tie!" shouted Dylan. The best friends high-fived each other and readied their flashlights for another round.

"You're too slow, Dyl," teased Ethan after winning three 'wars' in a row.

"I'll get you next time," warned Dylan. "I was just warming up."

"Are you two still interested in popcorn for a snack?" came Mrs. Nicholson's voice from the door of Ethan's room.

"Yes, please!" answered Ethan.

"Well, then, get your behinds out of that fort and go make it," said Mrs. Nicholson with a smile. "I've set up the popper in the kitchen."

"That is a *lot* of popcorn," said Dylan, as they poured a generous helping of butter over the humungous bowl of popcorn they had just popped. "It was only two handfuls of kernels."

Ethan grinned. "The more, the better."

"Guys, now would be a good time to change into your pyjamas," suggested Ethan's mom as they carried the popcorn into Ethan's room.

"Okie dokie," replied Ethan.

Minutes later, the boys were re-established in their fort, the bowl of popcorn between them.

"So, what happened last night? Why didn't you use our flashlight code?" Ethan asked.

Dylan flicked his flashlight on and off several times before speaking. It was comfortable and warm in the tent, his belly was full, and Ethan was looking at him kindly, calmly waiting for him to answer. Dylan knew Ethan was just curious and not angry with him for not communicating with him last night. Knowing Ethan was not annoyed with him made it easier to confide in him.

"Um, I was sort of in a bad mood," Dylan started explaining. "I didn't get in much trouble, my mom just kind of lectured me a little and said I was grounded if they got any more calls from Mrs. Cane. It's kinda weird, though, I wish I got in more trouble, 'cause it's almost like they hardly noticed I was there. Lucas threw two tantrums and Hailey was talking about a dance and being kinda rude, and Mom was getting annoyed with her and Dad was thinking about his book..." Dylan trailed off, twisting a corner of his pillow cover between his thumb and index finger.

Ethan nodded slowly. "Yeah, it sounds like they were totally distracted."

"Oh yeah, and my dad made this weird comment to my mom about the Wongs over on Biscayne losing their silver cutlery set. I think Dad said it was an heirloom or something. I feel like Dad and Mom aren't telling me everything. They sort of looked at each other funny before they told me what they meant when they were talking about the Wongs."

"Oooh, a mystery," crowed Ethan, gleefully rubbing his hands together. "And guess what else? I heard my mom talking on the phone to her friend and she was going on about somebody's garage being broken into."

Dylan had been lounging back on his pillow, but

now he sat up, his brown eyes lit with excitement. "Wouldn't it be great if we could figure out who's going around stealing stuff and breaking into garages?"

"Maybe we'd even get a reward!" exclaimed Ethan.

"Maybe we could figure out the other mystery of who's wrecking the park," added Dylan. "I bet if we did that, my parents would be totally proud of me and Hailey wouldn't treat me like I'm still six years old."

Ethan lay back on his sleeping bag and laced his fingers behind his head. "Real detectives start by making notes on suspects and stuff," he yawned. "Let's do that tomorrow morning."

Dylan took another handful of popcorn and a large sip from his water bottle. He wasn't ready to sleep yet. His mind was racing with the possibilities of solving a real mystery. His parents and Hailey would be sure to take notice of him then!

It was quiet for several minutes in the tent as Dylan thought about the five all important questions detectives needed to ask themselves: *Who* could be the criminal? *Why* were they doing it? *How* were they doing it? *When* were they committing the crimes? *Where* would they strike next?

Dylan was so deep in thought, he startled and knocked the bowl of popcorn over when Ethan's mom stuck her head in the fort. "Guys, it's time to put the snacks away and brush your teeth."

"Sure, Mom," answered Ethan sleepily, as he fumbled his way out of his sleeping bag and out of the fort.

Dylan hastily righted the bowl and scooped the spilled popcorn into it before following his best friend into the washroom.

"Ow," exclaimed Ethan as the boys were crawling back into their sleeping bags after brushing their teeth. "Popcorn kernels are harder than they look," he grumbled, rubbing his hand.

"Sorry," replied Dylan. "I guess I didn't get all the kernels picked up. I jumped when your mom asked us to brush our teeth. Sometimes I wish our house was as quiet as yours." Dylan's voice dropped to a whisper. "I worry Mom and Dad will adopt even more kids and then it'll be loud all the time and they'll have even less time for me."

"You could tell your parents how you feel," suggested Ethan. "I know they'll listen to you."

The boys lay quietly for a few minutes as Dylan thought about what Ethan said. It was true, his parents were good listeners once he had their undivided attention. "You're right."

Ethan spoke wistfully. "Sometimes I wish my house were as loud as yours."

Dylan reached for Ethan's hand. Dylan wasn't sure how to respond to his friend's sad comment. When the boys linked their fingers together, however, they could show support for one another, even when they didn't know what to say. It was just Ethan and his mother. Ethan's dad had left the family shortly after Ethan's fourth birthday. Ethan would occasionally get a card from his father, but that was all. Dylan knew how much Ethan missed having a dad.

Ethan squeezed Dylan's hand once. "Goodnight, Dylan."

"'Night," yawned Dylan.

Dylan lay awake for a long time, listening to the deep, even breathing of his best friend, as he thought about how he and Ethan could solve the mysteries of the vandalism at the park and the crimes in their neighbourhood.

CHAPTER FOUR

The next morning Dylan's mom picked him up from Ethan's.

"We're heading to the mall," explained Alexandra as they walked to the car. She unlocked the doors on their green station wagon. "We need groceries and I want to catch the sale at Shopper's Drug Mart."

Dylan climbed into the backseat and fastened his seat belt. "Are Lucas and Hailey coming?"

"Hailey is at home doing homework, and Dad and Lucas are at that indoor playground near the movie theatre," answered his mother, glancing in the rear-view mirror at him. "Is your seat belt on properly, Dyl? I didn't hear it click."

Dylan was happy to have some time alone, just him and his mom, but his good mood started to evaporate after she asked him about his seat belt. She was treating him like he was still six years old. Of course he knew how to put his seat belt on properly! He wanted to remind her he was nine years old, not six, but he was afraid if he said that, it would come out all whiny. He needed to prove he was more mature now and not such a little boy. He and Ethan had woken up early and discussed ways his mom and dad could notice him more and not treat him like a young child. Not whining, and speaking calmly, had been top of their list.

With that morning's conversation in mind, Dylan made his voice as polite as possible. "Yes, Mom, it's clicked in all the way."

His mom smiled. "Great." She backed the car out of the driveway and they made the short drive to the nearby mall. On the way there, Dylan took the list out of his pocket that he and Ethan had made after breakfast and reread it. There were only a few items on it: a notebook, pen, Scotch tape, magnifying glass, and walkie-talkies. Ethan had reminded Dylan not to ask for the walkie-talkies from Toys R Us because they broke easily and didn't have a very long range. They only worked when the boys were close together. He hoped his mother would agree to buying most, if not all of the items on his list. Dylan smiled as he remembered Ethan talking excitedly about all the things a good detective needed for solving mysteries. By the time their list was complete, there was hardly any room to sit on Ethan's bed there were so many *Hardy Boys*, *Encyclopedia Brown*, and *A to Z Mysteries* books all over it. As they added items to the list, Ethan would pull a book off his shelf, flip to a page, and point out examples of different types of magnifying glasses, or different ways to fingerprint using common household items like Scotch tape and flour.

Dylan tucked the list back into his pocket as his

mother parked at the entrance nearest the grocery store. "We'll start at the drugstore first, then head into Metro," she announced as they headed into the mall. "It's a shame what those vandals are doing to the park. Lucas won't last as long at an indoor play place as he does at the park."

Dylan nodded, hurrying to keep up with Alexandra's brisk pace. He knew his mother was referring to the fact that after a while, all the kids and the noise of the playland would start to overwhelm Lucas, and he would have a meltdown if they didn't get him out of there quickly.

"I'll carry the basket," volunteered Dylan once they were in the drugstore.

"Thank you, Dylan," answered his mom, ruffling his hair. "It's great to have a little helper with me today."

Dylan's smile faded and he felt bristly inside. He wasn't little! He was nine, going on ten—double digits—in the spring! Again, he bit his tongue and hurried to keep up with his mom, who was headed into the aisle with the pain relievers. It would not be a good idea to annoy his mom by complaining that she kept treating him like a little kid just before asking her for some of the stuff on his list.

"You still like the berry flavour, right?" his mom asked, her hand on the largest of the liquid Children's Advil containers on the shelf.

Dylan nodded, keeping his frown hidden from his mom by staring down at the floor. How could she even wonder about that? He hated all the other flavours, *especially* the grape kind. Back in grade one, he'd choked on a grape gobstopper out of his Halloween treat bag. His mom had used her first aid skills to help him spit out the candy. It had been the worst, most scary feeling ever. After that, he hated everything grape flavoured. Dylan worried as he followed his mom up and down the aisles. What was his mom going to forget about him next? His favourite colour? Green. His favourite food? Macaroni and cheese. His favourite movie of all time? The Disney *Planes* movie. He felt sad she was so busy with Lucas and Hailey she seemed to be forgetting about him.

Dylan shifted the basket from one hand to the other and pulled his wish list out of his pocket. It was more important than ever that he get the things he needed to solve those mysteries in the neighbourhood, to prove how mature and grown up he was.

"Mom," he began hesitantly, "I really need some notebooks with the spiral thingies on top, some Scotch tape, and a magnifying glass for my detective work."

"Oh, how cute. You're dressing up as a detective for Halloween. We've got plenty of Scotch tape at home, but we can get the notebooks and magnifying glass at Dollarama for much less than what they charge at Shopper's."

Dylan's relief that his mom was willing to buy two of the things on his list was soured by her 'how cute' comment. He wanted to be a real police detective when he grew up. He didn't want those things for a costume! He wanted them for real! She was talking down to him. Again!

Dylan tried not to let his grumpy feeling take over as he helped his mom unload the basket at the cash register. He reminded himself he was getting at least some of the things he wanted. His mom paid for the purchases and they headed into the dollar store, conveniently located just across the walkway from the drugstore.

"There they are, Mom," Dylan exclaimed happily as he pulled a package with four of the exact kind of notebook he wanted off the hook.

"Excellent!" his mom answered, glancing at her watch. "Let's go find that magnifying glass. Oh, and a new padlock," she continued. "Those'll be in the hardware section."

After paying for the magnifying glass, lock, and notebooks, Dylan and his mom began the walk through the mall to the grocery store. It was located at the other end of the mall from the dollar store. As they walked, Dylan thought about the best, most polite way to ask for the walkie-talkies on his list. They were the most important item on it. Ethan had reminded Dylan that a good detective always has a way of calling for backup. They could have used Ethan's, but they were broken. He *had* to have those walkie-talkies, but his mother was walking awfully quickly.

"Mom, how come you're in such a hurry?" asked Dylan, trying hard to stay calm. "Can't Dad look after Lucas a little longer?"

"Normally, yes, but now his publisher is expecting him to submit the first half of his book by next month. Dad needs all the time he can get to meet the deadline. The sooner we get home, the sooner I can help him with Lucas so Dad will have some free time to write."

They were nearing the technology store and although Dylan knew how much of a hurry they were in, he took a deep breath and turned to his mother. "Mom, Ethan's walkie-talkies broke and we really need new ones to be detectives and it'll only take a second to get them from the store. I'll pay you back when I've saved up enough..."

His mother cut him off. "No, now is not the time for making extra, last minute purchases, especially not from that overpriced, techie gadget store. We'll talk about it tonight after dinner. Halloween isn't for another three weeks."

Alexandra continued toward the grocery store, but Dylan remained standing in front of the technology store. He *needed* those walkie-talkies! If they weren't in such a rush, he knew he could have taken a minute to figure out the best words to describe to his mom his feelings about the walkie-talkies and about being a detective *for real.* But now, pressed for time, and feeling angrier and angrier, Dylan stomped his foot and called "Mom, wait!"

Dylan's mom stopped, turned, and came back to where he was standing, her eyes flashing with annoyance. "Dylan, what are you *doing?*

Dylan felt like Lucas probably did right before a tantrum. His heart was pounding, his fists were clenched, and he wanted to stomp his feet again, and jump up and down, and yell to relieve the stress he was feeling. Instead, he went to his last resort. "Pleeease, Mom, pretty pleeease, will you buy me the walkie-talkies?" Begging had sometimes worked for him when he was younger and he hoped it would now. Anyways, if he was being treated like a six-year-old, maybe he could at least get what he wanted out of it.

His mother's voice got lower and she spoke slowly and deliberately. "I have told you no, and standing there whining at me is *not* going to turn that *no* into a *yes,* and if you don't turn your attitude around right now, we won't even discuss those walkie-talkies at Meeting and Game Night tonight."

Being a member of the Marcotte family meant that every Saturday night, Dylan, Lucas, and Hailey gathered in the living room with their parents to participate in a family meeting. The meeting was a chance for everyone to bring up topics of interest or concern. The meeting always concluded with a discussion of the upcoming weekly schedule that would be posted on the fridge. After that, they got to play a board game. Dylan liked the game part of Meeting and Game Night the best.

Dylan's stomach hurt. His mom was really angry with him. She'd used the tone Hailey sometimes referred to as the 'stop dead in your tracks or else' voice. He hadn't meant to make her angry. Now he'd spoiled his chance of his mother seeing that he was more mature and grown up.

Dylan hung his head. He felt ashamed of his behaviour. He knew he'd disappointed her. "Sorry, Mom."

Alexandra knelt by her son and hugged him. "I know you are. I love you; I don't love that behaviour I just saw." She stood and brushed a stray hair out of his eyes. "Come on, buddy, let's get the shopping done."

Although his mom had accepted his apology, Dylan continued to feel bad as they walked through the grocery store filling their cart with food for the week ahead. He felt like he'd taken several steps backwards toward the goal of showing her how grown up and responsible he was. He'd accomplished one thing, though, he thought grimly, he'd gotten himself noticed! But it was the wrong kind of attention. His tummy had been starting to settle, but at that thought, his insides started to twist and turn again.

"Dyl, would you get the toilet paper out from under the cart, please, and put it on the belt?" asked his mom, interrupting his thoughts.

Dylan looked up. They were already at the checkout! "Okay," he answered, and reached down to pick up the bathroom tissue.

He placed the toilet paper on the conveyer belt and looked around. His mom always used the widest checkout lane that was nearest the exit. She said she liked the extra space that lane gave her for manoeuvring the cart in and unloading it. Beside them was the express lane. As Dylan glanced over at the people lined up there, he noticed a guy in shorts and a T-shirt. It was not that cold in October, but it wasn't shorts and T-shirt weather! He was about to poke his mom and point the guy out to her when he noticed what was in his basket. Three jars of peanut butter! Three! Who needed that much peanut butter? Dylan felt goosebumps break out all over his arms as he thought about who could possibly want so much peanut butter. The guy who was vandalizing the park, that's who!

CHAPTER FIVE

Dylan tugged urgently on his mom's purse strap to get her attention. "Mom, Mom, look at what that guy in the express has!" he whispered loudly, pointing in the direction of the young man in shorts.

"Dylan, honestly, what has gotten into you?" asked Alexandra as she put the last item from their cart onto the conveyer belt. "It's rude to point like that," she admonished him.

"But, Mom, he's got a lot of peanut butter," persisted Dylan, a little more loudly.

"Yup, peanut butter's on sale this week, a buck fifty off," said the cashier, who'd overheard Dylan.

His mom looked over at the guy in the express lane. "Yes, and he's got bread and jam, too. Probably a starving university student living on PB and J sandwiches." Alexandra turned to the cashier. "Sorry, my son's got an overactive imagination today."

"No worries," smiled the cashier. "It's so cute, him checking out what other people are buying."

"Cute's not the word I would use," responded his mom with a wry grin.

As his mom paid for the groceries and they loaded the cart with their bags, Dylan tried to keep an eye on 'peanut butter guy.' He needed to remember all the important details about what he looked like so when they got home, he could write down the facts in his new notebook. His mother didn't think that guy was suspicious, but Dylan did. If that guy was so into PB and J sandwiches, why didn't he also have three jars of jam in his basket? He was probably buying the bread and jam so he didn't look suspicious buying just peanut butter.

Dylan spent the ride home from the grocery store repeating the facts he wanted to remember about the guy quietly to himself. As soon as they got in the door with their purchases, he tossed his jacket in the direction of the closet, hastily kicked his shoes off, and headed to his room, the dollar store bag in his hand.

"Dylan, you can play with your magnifying glass and notebooks later, but right now I need your help unpacking the groceries," said his mother as she slid her purse off her shoulder and shrugged out of her jacket.

"Okay, I'll just put the bag in my room," Dylan answered, trying not to sigh. It wasn't *playing*; it was serious detective *work* he needed to get to! Putting away the groceries was going to take forever and he really wanted to write his notes *now* while they were still fresh in his mind.

Dylan was hanging up the cloth bags they used for grocery shopping when Lucas and David came home from the indoor playground.

"That place is an absolute madhouse," said David, helping Lucas unzip his jacket. "Hi, Dylan, did you have a good time at Ethan's?"

"Yeah, we made a blanket fort and slept in it," he answered.

Dylan's dad gave a quick nod in Dylan's direction, while reaching into his jacket pocket. He took Lucas' hearing aid out of it. "Alexandra, can you put this back on him? He pulled it off as we were leaving and he wouldn't hold still long enough for me to do it."

"No problem." Alexandra took the hearing aid and pulled Lucas in for a hug. "Let's sit on the couch for a minute," she said and signed to Lucas.

"Did he have a huge meltdown?" asked Alexandra as she settled herself on the sofa with Lucas in her lap.

"Not too bad; it started just as we were making our way through the crowds to pick up our shoes," David replied.

Dylan was sure his dad hadn't heard anything he'd said. He probably could have talked about riding big pink elephants in Ethan's backyard and his dad wouldn't have noticed. Dejected, Dylan walked slowly to his room. Once he solved the mysteries of the vandalism at the park and the thefts in their neighbourhood, *then* his parents would notice him for sure.

Dylan took the notebooks and magnifying glass out of the bag, sat down on his bed, and started writing. He made sure to print everything as neatly as he could. He even used his dictionary to look up words like *suspect* and *groceries* and *evidence* to make sure they were spelled correctly. If the police ever needed his notes, they would be able to read them easily. They would be impressed by how neat and organized they were.

He was rereading his description of the 'suspect,' as he now thought of that guy buying all the peanut butter, when Hailey knocked on his door, calling him for supper. Dylan tucked his notebook into his nightstand and went to the bathroom to wash his hands for supper.

"But I *gave* you the plastic spoon you like," Hailey was saying loudly as Dylan walked into the kitchen. "See?" Lucas was gesturing at the dishwasher and Hailey was waving a green plastic utensil at him.

Lucas had been shopping with Alexandra one day and had caught sight of a display of brightly coloured utensils known as sporks: spoon on one end, a fork on the other, and since they were on sale, Alexandra had bought several for Lucas, seeing how fascinated he was with them. Only now, Lucas would *only* eat with a spork, nothing else would do.

David was tapping away on his keyboard and Alexandra was out in the garden, emptying the compost container. Lucas started jumping up and down and yelling.

"Dylan," pleaded Hailey, turning to her brother, "can you figure out what Thing Two wants before he goes completely crazy?"

Dylan thought he knew what the problem was. It wasn't about the kind of utensil; it was about the colour. In the last week, Dylan had noticed Lucas lining up all the blue Legos when he was playing and preferring to drink out of the blue plastic cup, and of course, Thomas the Tank Engine was blue. Lucas was a smart little boy. He probably guessed that if there weren't blue sporks in the drawer, then there were some in the dishwasher.

Dylan opened the dishwasher and took out a blue spork. He rinsed it in the sink and was handing it to Lucas as Alexandra came into the kitchen with the empty compost bucket.

"David, let's eat!" called Alexandra to her husband as they all took their places at the table.

Hailey grinned at Dylan. "I think I'm going to call you the 'Thing Two Whisperer.'"

Dylan wasn't sure what Hailey meant by her comment, but he felt like it was better than being called Thing One.

After dinner, everyone settled into their favourite comfortable spots in the living room for the weekly meeting. Lucas was wedged between David and Alexandra on the couch, Hailey was sitting cross-legged on the floor by the coffee table, and Dylan lounged in the easy chair next to the sofa.

"First order of business, and the most important one," began David. "The park is still off-limits until they find the person or people responsible for the vandalism. In the meantime, you can use the swing set in the backyard." He looked meaningfully at Hailey and Dylan. "This rule is non-negotiable," he continued sternly.

Dylan nodded like he understood, but he didn't. His dad was always using big words and was happy to tell his children what they meant, but today Dylan didn't want to ask. He wanted his dad to see him as older and mature, like a boy who understood things and didn't need to have words like 'non-negotiable' explained to him.

Alexandra turned to Lucas and signed, "No park. Still broken. Use swing. Backyard."

Dylan smiled when Lucas nodded and signed, "kay." For a brief moment, he wished all talking could be as straight forward as he found sign language to be. It made sense to him and he was comfortable with it, finding it fun. Dylan's mom had used seven words to replace all the big words his father had been using. It was the same message, only shorter and easier to understand.

"All right, does anyone have any comments, questions, or concerns tonight?" asked David.

Hearing his dad talk about the park being off-limits renewed Dylan's resolve to figure out who was wrecking their beloved park beside the little forest. The time had come to ask for the walkie-talkies. Dylan crossed his fingers for luck and took a deep breath. "Can I have a walkie-talkie? Ethan's broke and we need it for being detectives."

David looked over at Alexandra. "What do you think?"

"I guess there's no harm in Googling them to see how much they cost," answered Alexandra. She looked over at Dylan. "We're just price checking right now," she cautioned.

Dylan nodded, and David opened his laptop. "Hmm," he said after a minute of typing and scrolling.

Alexandra leaned across Lucas to look at the screen on the laptop. "They're on sale at Toys R Us this week," she commented.

"But," began Dylan, "the ones from Toys R Us don't work very well. We need walkies that work when Ethan and I are far apart."

Dylan's dad ran a hand through his dark hair. "I'll check a few more sites, but I'm not making any promises."

"Well," said Dylan's dad a few minutes later, looking up from the laptop. "The higher end walkie-talkies are referred to as 'two-way radios' and they're going to run us well over a hundred dollars, not including the tax."

"Sorry, Dyl, that's just too expensive a toy for your detective Halloween costume," said Dylan's mom.

Dylan rubbed at his eyes in an effort to stop the tears from leaking out. He couldn't cry now. They would just think of him even more as a six-year-old, and not an almost ten-year-old. It was hard, though. How were he and Ethan going to do their detective work without a way of communicating with each other at times when they couldn't see each other? Dylan didn't have a cell phone to use. He had asked for one for his ninth birthday, but his parents had told him he had to wait at least two more years before he could get one.

"Sure, okay," mumbled Dylan. He tucked his feet under him and thought about how to be a detective without a phone or a walkie-talkie.

"Hey, Mom," said Hailey. "Can I upgrade my phone to an iPhone 7?"

Alexandra looked startled. "Is your phone broken?"

"Well, no, it's just that Samantha and Julie, and, like, practically everyone else in grade nine has one," Hailey said, her voice trailing off into a mumble.

"That's no reason to want such an expensive phone," replied David. "Your phone works fine now. Your mom and I don't buy into that nonsense about always having the latest gadget. It's wasteful and not environmentally friendly at all to just throw away something because it's not new enough."

"But," continued Hailey, crossing her arms and glaring at her parents. "I've had my phone for three years; it's practically a dinosaur."

"The answer is no, Hailey," said Alexandra firmly. "I'm sorry to disappoint you, but I agree with your dad. You will have to make do with your perfectly useable phone. We might live in a throw-away society, but we don't support it."

"Fine," said Hailey angrily. "Whatever, I guess I'll just have to..."

"Stop speaking right now," interrupted Alexandra. "Your tone and attitude are becoming unacceptable," she warned.

Lucas jumped off the couch and ran to the shelf where they kept the games. He pulled out Hungry Hungry Hippos and set it down with a *thunk* on the coffee table.

"Okay, okay," laughed David, looking over at Hailey who was staring down at the carpet and frowning deeply. "It's definitely time for something fun. I'll just go over next week's schedule before we start the game."

Dylan knew it was mean, but he felt a little bit satisfied that Hailey wasn't getting what she wanted tonight either. At least she *had* a phone! As their dad went over the week's coming events, Dylan started to make some plans.

While Dylan's dad was setting up the Hungry Hungry Hippos game, Dylan continued to think. He was glad it was a game that didn't need a lot of concentration. You just had to push a lever to make your hippo open its mouth to try and catch the most marbles. Dylan absent-mindedly jabbed at the lever on his red hippo to make it catch marbles as some ideas started to come to him. If he was going to investigate for clues at the park, he needed to find a way to get around the rule of not being allowed to go to the park. But in order to sneak to the park, he would have to break the number one rule in his family of always telling the truth.

Hailey elbowed Dylan, jarring him back to reality.

"Game's over; Lucas and I won. We're going for best of three," she informed him.

Dylan pried the marbles he had caught out of his hippo's mouth and returned them to the middle of the plastic game board. His tummy was starting to feel jumpy as he thought about his other idea. It went against another family rule of not touching things that weren't yours. He didn't like being dishonest, but, Dylan reasoned with himself, it would all be worth it when he discovered who the bad guy in the neighbourhood was. A good detective *always* had a way of calling for backup and a camera for taking pictures for evidence. Hailey had a phone she didn't even want! Even though she thought it was old, she was never far from it. How was he going to sneak into her room to take her phone to use when he was collecting clues at the park he was forbidden to go to?

CHAPTER SIX

"Come on, just admit it. You hated it," said Ethan. It was Monday, and Dylan and Ethan were sitting outside on the grass near the baseball diamond at lunch.

Dylan snapped the lid shut on his empty plastic sandwich container and tucked it carefully into his nylon lunch bag. He pulled an apple out of his lunch bag and took a huge bite. While he chewed, he thought about what he wanted to say to his best friend. This morning before the first bell, Dylan had started to take the peanut butter suspect description out of his pocket to share with Ethan, when Ethan had excitedly shown him a book he had found at the library.

"It's Morse code," Ethan had explained. "The most famous code of all!" Ethan had flipped open the book to show Dylan how the code worked. All Dylan had seen was a page full of little dots and dashes next to the letters of the alphabet, numbers, and even punctuation marks like question marks, and commas. It had looked very complicated and Dylan knew there was no way he could learn to use a code like that! Ethan had chattered on and on about the code and how it was made up of sounds, and Dylan had become more and more quiet. Ethan had even used a stick to tap out an example of how to call for help using Morse code. Dylan wanted to ask why the call for help used the letters S O S, when that wasn't how you spelled the word *help*, but he couldn't squeeze a word in sideways, Ethan was speaking so quickly. As Dylan tried to make sense of the page Ethan was showing him, he couldn't help but start to feel very stupid and very insecure. He wished he could learn new things as quickly as Ethan did. He really wanted to be as enthusiastic about the code as Ethan was and he felt like he was letting his best friend down by not wanting to use the new code.

Dylan shrugged. "I didn't hate it, exactly. It looked very confusing. There's a lot to remember."

Ethan nodded. "True, but we don't have to learn it all at once. We could learn a bit at a time." He grinned at Dylan. "I just had the best idea. We could learn five letters every Friday at our sleepovers." Ethan's grin faded as he glanced at Dylan. "Would you want to do that?"

"Yeah," mumbled Dylan, looking down and brushing his fingers back and forth through the grass. "I guess." Ethan probably already knew the whole code and Dylan felt like he was the dumb kid slowing his smart friend down. That code was going to be impossible to learn, but what kind of a friend would he be if he didn't at least try?

"Great," replied Ethan, taking a granola bar out of his lunch bag.

As Dylan watched Ethan tearing the wrapper

clearly marked with the 'peanut free' symbol, he suddenly thought of the peanut butter suspect he had seen on Saturday. He felt happy to talk about something other than that code. He pulled the notebook with his description of the peanut butter suspect out of his pocket.

"Check this out," he said, opening the notebook to the first page and passing it to Ethan. "Look what I saw when I was getting groceries with my mom."

Ethan studied Dylan's notes and frowned. "Yeah, that's definitely suspicious. So, we have to keep an eye out for a tall, skinny guy with super short brown hair and three silver hoops in his left ear. Someone like that should be easy to spot," said Ethan confidently. He handed the notebook back to Dylan. "Nice notebook. It looks official. Did your mom get you the walkie-talkies and the magnifying glass?"

"She got me the magnifying glass, but her and Dad say the walkies are too expensive," groaned Dylan.

"Oh," moaned Ethan. "That sucks. My mom won't get them for us right now either. She said I should put them on my Christmas wish list, but that's no good for now."

"I've been thinking about what we can do instead of the walkie-talkies," began Dylan. At that moment, the bell rang, signalling the end of lunch.

"Cool. We'll talk about it on the way home," replied Ethan, brightening.

As the boys picked up their lunch bags and headed into the school, Dylan hoped Ethan would agree to his plan. Dylan felt that coming up with a great plan his best friend loved would make up for his not being so excited to learn Morse code.

On the walk home from school that afternoon, Dylan outlined his plan of sneaking the phone out of Hailey's room.

"What if she catches you?" asked Ethan with a worried look.

"I'll just wait 'til she goes to the bathroom," answered Dylan. "She always takes forever in there. I only need a minute to get in, grab it, and get out."

Ethan still looked worried. "Wouldn't it be easier if you just asked her to borrow her phone? Then you wouldn't have to sneak around."

Dylan sighed. "The last time I asked her to use her phone she said no. Besides, she'll want to know what I want it for and I'll have to make something up. So, either way, I still have to be sneaky."

"I guess," agreed Ethan reluctantly. "We still have to figure out our other problem of looking around at the park. My mom is going to freak if she finds out I went to the park."

"Yeah, mine too," said Dylan.

The boys fell silent.

"What about if we go to the park on Friday?"

proposed Ethan thoughtfully. "It's my turn at your house for the sleepover. We could wait for Hailey to go to the washroom, get the phone, then go to the park." Ethan rubbed his hands together gleefully as he expanded on the plan. "We could tell your dad we're looking for something that fell out of my backpack on the way home from school."

"Yeah, and my dad's so busy writing his novel and keeping Lucas busy, he won't notice if we're gone a bit longer," added Dylan. "Oh, and you should be the look-out! That way you won't have to go near the climbers and stuff, in case there's peanut butter around."

"Hey, this is going to be fun," said Ethan. "But we have to be safe. If I'm the look-out, we need a way for me to signal you if there's danger."

Dylan nodded. "It would be great if we could use our flashlights, but it won't be dark enough and we'd have to be able to see each other the whole time."

"No, flashlights won't work, but some sort of loud sound only you and I know the meaning of would work," mused Ethan.

"What about if you clapped your hands really loudly?" suggested Dylan. "I would understand that."

"Nah, the bad guys would know there are people around if they heard someone clap their hands," replied Ethan as they approached his house. "We don't want them to know we're there."

"Well, we still have a few days to figure it out," said Dylan as he watched Lucas ran down their driveway to greet him.

"See ya tomorrow," called Ethan as he headed up the walkway to his house.

Dylan swooped his little brother into a tight hug. Lucas could be such a pain sometimes, but he always gave the best hugs. Dylan smiled as Lucas led him into the house.

That evening after dinner, Dylan sat at his desk and twirled his magnifying glass around as he thought about how Ethan could secretly, but loudly, let him know if there was danger at the park when they were investigating for clues. What was a loud sound that didn't sound like a person had made it? Some kind of animal sound maybe? Dylan sat at his desk a long time, thinking. His mom had put Lucas to bed for the night and it was so quiet he could hear the rapid clack of the keys as his dad wrote his novel. He could hear Hailey humming along with her favourite Katy Perry CD. He could even hear the birds chirping outside as they settled into the trees for the night.

And that's when it came to him. He knew *exactly* how Ethan could signal him if there was danger at the park!

CHAPTER SEVEN

Dylan was reaching for the portable phone on his desk to phone Ethan when his mother came into the room. "Dyl? You know it's too late to be calling Ethan now."

Dylan glanced over at his bedside digital clock. "But Mom, it's only 8:45," he said, his voice sounding way more whiny than he wanted.

"You know how I feel about a good night's rest for everyone in this family, including you," she replied, pulling his pyjamas out of his drawer. "What's so important you have to call him now?"

Dylan's stomach twisted. He always told his mom everything. What was he going to say? He couldn't tell her about the secret signal system he had thought of; she'd want to know what it was for and there was no way he could explain that. The whole secret plan to explore the park would be over before it even started! He said the first thing he could think of. "Uh, I was just asking him for help with math," he mumbled.

"I asked you at supper if you had finished your homework, and you told me you did," answered his mother. "Did you lie to me?"

Uh oh! This conversation was going from bad to worse! "No!" he replied emphatically, on the verge of shouting. "I mean, no," he continued more softly. "I guess I forgot about this one question and I remembered it a few minutes ago and I tried to do it and I was having trouble, so I thought I'd call Ethan for help."

"Okay, where's this question? Maybe I can help," said his mother, glancing over at his desk.

"Actually, it was extra, for bonus marks, and I thought maybe I could do it," continued Dylan, adding another lie to his growing list. "It's okay, though, I don't have to do it."

He sat down on his bed and started to take off his socks. He remembered his mom lecturing Hailey that time she had been caught cheating on a test. "It won't ever be just one lie, Hailey," she had said. "You'll always end up having to cover up the first lie with another lie." Dylan hadn't understood it at the time, but now he sure did. He'd just told three lies in a row.

His mom sat down beside him. She didn't look convinced by anything he'd said. "You're trying to cover something up and I'd like to know..."

"Mom, can you make me a hot water bottle? My stomach hurts." Hailey was standing at the door to his room, holding her stomach.

"Sure, honey." His mom got up to help Hailey. "I'll be back in to say good night, Dylan," she said as she left his room.

By the time Dylan's mom returned to his room to say good night, he had already brushed his teeth, gotten into his pyjamas, and was in bed, pretending to be asleep. He felt awful deceiving her, but it was the only way he could think of to avoid the conversation she wanted to have. It took him a long time to fall asleep. He debated whether he should just tell her everything, and get her help solving the mysteries of the park and the thief in the neighbourhood. But she was so busy and so were Dad and Hailey. And what if they said no, he wasn't allowed to do any detective work because they thought it would be too dangerous? By the time Dylan fell asleep, he had decided not to ask his parents for help. He knew if he helped catch the bad guys in the neighbourhood, they would finally see how grown up and smart he was, and they would pay more attention to him. Most importantly, they would be proud of him.

The next morning Dylan woke up early. When he glanced out his window, he could see it was still dark out. He glanced over at the clock on his nightstand. It was 6:30 in the morning. Dylan snuggled down deeper into his covers. He didn't need to get up for another hour.

He was thinking about what to say if his mom asked him more about their talk last night when he heard Hailey leave her room to go into the bathroom. So Hailey was up earlier than usual today, too.

Dylan briefly entertained the idea of getting up,

but it was just too cozy to leave his bed so soon. The smell of toast and coffee drifted in from the kitchen, as well as the low voices of his parents, along with the clattering of dishes. Lucas was always the first awake and ate his breakfast long before Dylan and Hailey did.

He laced his hands behind his head and thought about how to explain his phone call with Ethan in a way that would satisfy his mother while not giving anything away about his sleuthing plans. He had decided he would just admit he couldn't wait to tell Ethan about a code he had thought of, when he heard his sister loudly complaining.

"But Mom, I don't have time to clear the table now," she said, her voice a plaintive whine. "I was gonna meet Samantha and Julie early to cram for our history test."

"You'll take a minute to wipe down and clear the table, please," he heard his mother reply in a no-nonsense tone. "Julie and Samantha can wait."

At the sound of Hailey's disgruntled "fine," and the clattering of dishes being put into the dishwasher, Dylan figured he might as well get out of bed. He dawdled around in his room for several minutes, taking his time getting dressed. Hailey was in a grumpy mood and he'd just as soon not cross paths with her.

Ten minutes later, when he heard his sister holler "Bye," and the front door open and then slam shut, he left his room to use the washroom.

After washing his face and brushing his teeth, he returned to his room to pick up his backpack. He was zipping his bag shut when he heard his dad rap lightly on his open door.

"Oh good, you're up," he said. "Do you know where Lucas' blankie might be? Your mom and I can't find it, and Lucas is on the verge of a meltdown."

Lucas' blankie wasn't actually a blanket. It was a thin square of white cotton, about the size of a washcloth, edged in a pale-yellow satin border. Lucas had brought it with him when he had come to live with them, and in those first few months he had constantly clutched his security blanket. It was only in the last several months that Lucas had become comfortable enough to put his beloved blankie down during meals, or when he was playing.

"Did you check the laundry?" asked Dylan.

"Not yet," answered his dad. "I thought he had it with him at breakfast, but it's not on the table."

"Maybe he left it in my room," suggested Dylan.

"I'll look in the washing machine," responded Dylan's dad, striding off down the hall.

As Dylan searched his room for the blanket, he thought of that *Franklin the Turtle* storybook he had loved when he was younger. In the story, Franklin had also lost his security blanket. The blanket had eventually been found under a chair in the kitchen. The turtle had used it to hide some green vegetable he hadn't wanted to eat at supper. The story gave Dylan an idea. Maybe Lucas' blanket was somewhere in the kitchen and his parents just hadn't found it.

Dylan headed to the kitchen and when he got there, he saw that Lucas had progressed from being on the verge of a meltdown to a full temper tantrum. His little brother was sprawled out on the kitchen floor, kicking and flailing. As Dylan scanned the area under the table for the blanket, he noticed Lucas' hearing aid on the floor near Hailey's chair. When Lucas got really upset, he always ripped his hearing aid off. Dylan picked it up and handed it to his dad, who was kneeling by Lucas, gently cleaning the tears running down the distraught little boy's cheeks.

"Thanks," said his dad. "Your mom's turning the living room upside down looking for the blanket," he continued, getting up to dispose of the soiled tissue and to put the hearing aid on the counter.

"Can you pass me another tissue, Dad, please?" asked Dylan as he knelt beside Lucas, who was now curled into a ball and crying hard.

Dylan wiped the tears and snot from his brother's face. "We'll find blankie," he signed, and smoothed Lucas' hair out of his eyes. After a few minutes, Lucas started to calm down. His frantic sobbing turned into quiet snuffling.

Dylan got up to put the soiled Kleenex in the garbage can. The bag was full so Dylan pulled it out to replace it. It was wedged firmly, however, and Dylan had to give it several firm tugs. Suddenly, the bag flew out of the can and Dylan lost his grip on it. Trash spilled on to the floor.

"Great," muttered Dylan as he began cleaning up the mess. There, under several scrunched-up paper napkins, was Lucas' blankie! In her haste to leave the house and meet her friends, Hailey must have accidentally thrown out the blanket with the napkins as she cleared the table. Dylan quickly picked it up, shook it out over the kitchen sink, and gave it to Lucas. The blanket was dirty, but his dad could launder it today, probably when Lucas was watching a video and less likely to notice his blanket was in the wash.

"Thanks, you're a lifesaver," said his mom, who had come into the kitchen to wash her hands in the sink. "There are some wicked dust bunnies under the sofa," she joked.

"I don't know what we'd do without you," praised his dad.

Dylan shrugged, embarrassed. It wasn't such a big deal. He'd only found the blanket because he'd made a huge mess of trying to take out a garbage bag.

Dylan sat down at the table to eat a quick breakfast. As he was spooning in the last of the Cheerios, his dad reminded him that it was Meet the Teacher night at Hailey's school.

"Oh, yeah," said Dylan. "Do you think I could stay

home while you go? I'll be ten soon." It sounded really boring to follow his parents around as they went from class to class in Hailey's school, which was huge, just to meet all her teachers.

"No, you're too young for that," answered his dad, smiling sympathetically at him. "It'll only be an hour or so," he consoled Dylan.

Dylan put his empty cereal bowl in the sink with a loud thunk. He wasn't too young! He would only sit in the living room and watch TV while his parents were out. Dylan knew once he figured out who was wrecking the park and breaking into garages, his parents would *finally* see he wasn't a little kid anymore; he was a kid who could handle the responsibility of staying home alone for an hour or two. He *had* to solve those mysteries—soon!

CHAPTER EIGHT

D ylan spent the walk to school telling Ethan what he had thought of last night. "You know how in gym Mrs. Ramirez uses her whistle? One blast for stop where you are, and two blasts for everybody gathering back together so she can give us our next instructions?"

"Yeah," answered Ethan. "I think whistling still sounds too obvious..."

"I know," interrupted Dylan. "What if we make a whistle sound like birds calling to each other, or chirping or something?"

Ethan slowed as he thought. "You know, that might work! We could look up what different birds sound like and then pick a sound we can copy and use that!" Ethan high-fived Dylan. "That's a fantastic idea!"

Dylan grinned. He had come up with a great idea his best friend thought could work. It felt amazing to be able to contribute something creative and smart to their plan. Dylan couldn't stop smiling and the morning at school went quickly. At lunch as he was eating, he felt like his throat was a bit sore but he dismissed it. They had gym just before lunch on Tuesdays and his throat probably felt rough from all the running and laughing he had been doing during the dodgeball game.

That night at dinner, Dylan couldn't stop yawning as he picked listlessly at dinner. Usually, he loved his mom's meatloaf, but tonight he wasn't feeling very hungry.

"You okay, Little Man?" asked his mother as she looked over at him. "You've hardly eaten anything."

Dylan shrugged. He didn't trust himself to speak. He wanted to yell that he wasn't little anymore, but his head was starting to hurt and he didn't want to get into trouble for being rude.

"It's already 5:45," said his dad, glancing at the kitchen clock. "We'd better get a move on. Our first appointment is with your math teacher, Hailey, and that's in half an hour."

Dylan only managed a few more forkfuls of his supper before his parents were hustling him, Lucas, and Hailey out the door for the walk to the high school, where they would have an opportunity to meet all of Hailey's teachers for this semester.

Usually, when he went on a walk with his family, Dylan was way out in front, calling for everyone else to hurry up, but today, he didn't feel up to rushing. As he dawdled along behind his parents, aimlessly kicking leaves along the sidewalk, he caught a fragment of their conversation that made his heart start beating faster.

"... was telling me her daughter-in-law's car got broken into last night," said his mom, giving a quick glance behind her at Dylan. She lowered her voice and Dylan hurried to catch up to hear the rest of their conversation.

"Oh, wow," replied his dad. "Did she leave it locked?"

"Yeah, they smashed the driver's side window in. They took the GPS and a bunch of spare change out of the car."

"What did the police say? Do they think it's the same guy who's been doing all the other break-ins?"

"Mom!" hollered Hailey from behind Dylan. "If Lucas has to look at every single worm on the sidewalk we're going to be late! Can you help me hurry him up, please?"

Dylan stuffed his hands in his pockets and frowned as his mother went to help Hailey with his little brother. The conversation between his parents was just getting interesting! There was definitely a bad guy out there, stealing stuff, and it wasn't his first time stealing! Maybe that silverware set belonging to the Wongs wasn't really lost: it was stolen—by that bad guy! Dylan wished he had brought his detective notebook and a pen along. It would be really handy now!

They were entering the front doors of the school as Dylan continued to muse about what he had heard.

"Hi, Hailey!" chirped a friendly looking girl with long blond hair, who was standing with a clipboard just inside the front doors of the school. She turned to David and Alexandra. "Welcome to Parent Night. Do you need any help finding a particular class?"

"It's okay, I've got this," said Hailey with a quick smile at the bubbly teen as she led the way to a set of stairs on the right.

"Who was that?" asked Alexandra as they followed Hailey up the stairs.

"Oh, that's Amber; Miss Enthusiasm. She's in my English class. Can you believe she actually volunteered to stand in front of a door for two hours?" replied Hailey.

Hailey's math class was on the second floor, at the end of the corridor.

"Dylan, we only have a few minutes with each teacher, and I'm worried Lucas will become impatient and interrupt. We need you to be our 'Lucas wrangler,'" said Dylan's dad, gesturing at two chairs directly opposite the door to Hailey's math class.

Alexandra pulled several *Thomas* storybooks out of her bag and gave them to Dylan. "Those should keep Lucas occupied for a bit. Dad and I will be still able to see you and help if Lucas gets too fidgety."

Dylan gave a book to Lucas before sinking down in the chair. Hailey's school was so big! He hoped her other classes were close by. Maybe if he closed his eyes for a few minutes the itchy, burning feeling in them would go away. Within seconds, Dylan began to nod off.

"...should have seen that kid when he landed in the dog poop at the bottom of the slide."

Dylan was jerked awake from his snooze when he heard voices and laughter coming from just around the corner of the hallway on his right. He sat up quickly, rubbing his eyes. Lucas was still beside him, engrossed in a pop-up train book. He glanced around. At the far end of the hall to his left, he could see a father and daughter, both focused on their cell phones as they waited for their interview.

Had he heard something about dog poop? At the bottom of a slide? Dylan leaned forward on his chair, straining to hear more of what was being said.

"You've got nerve," Dylan heard someone with a deep voice say. "Sticking around like that? Where'd you hide so no one could see you?"

"Right out in the open," answered someone else with a rough voice. "I was just circling the parking lot on my skateboard, watching the whole thing." He laughed meanly. "Kids are so dumb. He was trying to wipe off his shoes with sand and shuffling through the grass to get the poop off. He looked so stupid. It was hilarious."

"Let me know when you're spreading the peanut butter around. That should be good for a laugh," replied the guy with the deep voice. "Anything's better than being forced to stay here, directing lost parents."

Dylan stood up quickly. Peanut butter guy from the store was here! All he had to do now was casually walk around the corner to see who the bad guys were!

"I gotta get rid of a silverware set," said the teen with the rough voice. "You wanna come with? I'm skipping off tomorrow to go downtown. See which pawn shop'll..."

At that moment, they were drowned out by the bell sounding, followed by a reminder over the P.A. that it was time to proceed to the next interview.

"Dylan!" called his mother, just as he was about to round the corner. "Where are you off to? You need to stay with Lucas!"

"Just a second, Mom!" said Dylan as he took the three steps he needed to see around the corner. He was so close! His mom would be annoyed with him for not coming right away, but he just had to see! It might be his only chance! Hopefully they would still be there, hiding out in the open like the one guy was bragging about.

But as he peeked around the corner, all he could see was a girl and her parents walking toward him. His 'suspects' had disappeared.

"Honestly, Dylan, what's gotten into you these days?" said his mother as she took him by the hand. "We're going to be late for our appointment with Hailey's English teacher if you keep playing games like this."

Dylan felt like he was six years old again as his mother towed him along toward the stairs. When they reached the staircase, he let go of her hand to hold the railing. She gave him a look. "We have three more appointments. No more shenanigans, Dylan." She was using the tone that meant she was at the end of her patience.

Dylan's stomach hurt and his head was starting to pound. His mouth was dry and his eyes felt like they were on fire. Dylan was starting to worry he was getting sick, and that meant a fever was not far behind. When his mother looked away he surreptitiously felt his forehead using the back of his hand, like she always did. Still cool. Okay, good.

As he and Lucas followed his parents around to meet Hailey's teachers, Dylan was planning. By the time they were on the walk home, he had decided that as soon as they got in the door, he would take some Advil. His mother usually helped him, but today he wanted to do it himself. He knew exactly how much to pour into the little plastic cup that came with the medicine. He would tell his parents after he'd taken the correct dose.

Dylan hurriedly hung up his jacket in the hall closet while kicking off his shoes the minute they arrived home. His parents were preoccupied with encouraging Lucas to leave the worms he had collected from their walk outside, and didn't see him dash into the bathroom. He was feeling way worse than when they left the high school. He felt shivery and cold and he knew he now had a fever.

He stepped up on to the foot stool Lucas always used, yanked open the mirrored medicine cabinet door over the sink, and grabbed the Advil container with a shaky hand. The bottle slipped out of his hand and bounced off the edge of the sink. Dylan lunged for it, but missed. The medicine landed on the floor and rolled behind the toilet. With a groan, Dylan reached down to pick up the container. He tried to twist the cap open, but it didn't budge. Of course! It was child-proof! Dylan tried to remember what his mother did. Did she squeeze the sides and turn? Or did she press down firmly on the top while twisting? Dylan tried several times to push and turn the lid. He was sweating now and his hands were clammy and trembling. He was ready to give up and ask for help when the lid suddenly popped off. The bottle flew out of his hand and berry-flavoured medicine spilled all down his shirt.

But it was too late. Dylan's arm started to jerk and his mouth filled with saliva. He felt tingly all over and everything was blurry. He knew in the millisecond before that he was going to have a seizure. Before he could finish that thought, Dylan felt himself falling and everything went black.

CHAPTER NINE

D ylan frowned as he looked in the mirror the following morning. He ran his fingers lightly along the bluish-purple bruise in the middle of his forehead. It was the size of a toonie and still felt tender when he touched it.

He stuck his tongue out at the mirror before looking away from his reflection. He sighed as he thought about how he'd made things even worse. In trying to do things himself, he'd made a complete mess, proving to his parents he *was* just a little kid who couldn't open a bottle. Last night, once he'd become conscious after the seizure, his mother had helped him get cleaned up and change into pyjamas. While his dad had driven to the pharmacy to pick up more medicine, Hailey had put Lucas to bed before mopping up the spilled medicine on the bathroom floor. When his dad returned with the Advil, his mom had given him a dose to bring his fever down.

Dylan sighed and rubbed his forehead. Just before tucking him in and kissing him goodnight, his mother had asked him if there was anything he wanted to talk about. He knew she was expecting him to tell her why he'd been trying to get the Advil himself without telling her he was feeling sick. Dylan had shut his eyes and shaken his head in response to his mother's quiet question. All his feelings about trying to prove he was mature and grown up so he could be noticed were jumbled and tangled up in a messy ball, like the Christmas lights were when they first unpacked them every year. He didn't even know how to begin explaining things to her so he took the easy way out, closed his eyes, and pretended to fall asleep.

Dylan tried and failed to suppress a huge yawn. Because he had bumped his head hard, his mom had woken him several times during the night to make sure he didn't have a concussion. He was trying to figure out what words to use to explain why he had been trying to get the Advil himself when Hailey knocked on the bathroom door he had left open.

"That bruise is not getting any better by looking at it," she said, squeezing past him. She looked at herself in the mirror, groaned, and elbowing him aside, opened the medicine cabinet. "I swear, this pimple is so big, it has its own heartbeat," she grumbled as she reached for her acne cover-up medication.

Dylan retreated to his room to get dressed. The one good thing, he supposed, about having a seizure, was that he would be staying home from school until he was better. It was Wednesday, and Mrs. Cane called Wednesdays 'wild.' She said they were wild because they were full of surprises. Sometimes the surprise was that they got to see a movie and have popcorn, but sometimes the surprise was a 'see if you've been paying attention' test on math or spelling. Dylan didn't like the test kind of surprise. He hoped the 'surprise' he would be missing today would be a math test.

"Dyl, breakfast is ready," said his mom as he was pulling a warm, cozy sweatshirt over his head. "You up to eating in the kitchen or do you want me to deliver?" she joked.

"I'm okay," fibbed Dylan. "I'll be there in a second." He would have liked to take his mother up on her offer to serve him breakfast on a tray in bed, but he didn't want her to have to baby him today. Alexandra preferred to take the day off work to monitor him after he had a seizure. She had been promoted to nurse manager at the hospital and had a bit more freedom to take time off. She'd explained this to Dylan several times, but he still sometimes felt guilty she was missing work because of him. Today he felt even worse because she was going to ask him about last night and he still didn't know what to say.

He slowly plodded out of his room toward the kitchen where his mother had buttered toast and juice waiting for him. He sat down at the table and took a small sip of the juice. His throat was still sore and his head still thumped, even though his mother had given him a dose of Advil right after he'd woken up.

Alexandra lightly brushed the back of her hand against his forehead. "Your fever's come down. That's good," she said. She ran her fingers through his hair, brushing his bangs aside to look at the bruise on his forehead. Dylan leaned into his mother's touch, enjoying the gentle feel of her fingers.

"You're going to be feeling that bump for a few days," his mother said, sitting down beside him.

He nodded, and took a bite of toast. The silence between Dylan and his mother grew as Dylan concentrated on eating the toast and drinking his orange juice. Hailey had left for school and David had taken Lucas for their usual walk around the neighbourhood to 'get the creative writing juices flowing,' as Dylan's dad always liked to joke.

"Do you want more toast?" asked Dylan's mother once he had eaten the last bite.

"No, thank you," answered Dylan, not looking at her. He had been eating as slowly as possible to put off the conversation he knew his mother wanted to have.

Dylan's mother pushed his empty plate and glass to the centre of the table and took both his hands in hers. "Look at me, Dylan, please."

Dylan dragged his gaze up to his mother's face.

"What's going on with you? You haven't seemed yourself these last few days."

Dylan's resolve not to tell her everything almost crumpled at that moment. He'd expected her to be angry with him for not telling her he was sick, and for taking medicine without adult supervision, and for making such a mess in the bathroom, but she just looked concerned and confused.

"I thought I could take the Advil by myself," he mumbled. "You and Dad were busy with Lucas and the worms."

"Oh, Dylan, you could have interrupted us. Or, at the very least, Hailey would have been glad to help you," she said, slowly rubbing the knuckles on his right hand with her thumb.

"Yeah, I know," answered Dylan. He felt awful.

"Dylan, part of growing up means learning that sometimes it's okay to do things on your own and sometimes it's also okay to ask for help," said his mother quietly.

Dylan slowly pulled his hands out from under his mother's as he thought about what she said. It had seemed like a good idea at the time, but looking back, he realized he should have asked for help. Just like Ethan, he had an important medical condition. For Ethan, managing that condition meant being responsible and having his life-saving medication with him at all times. For Dylan, managing his seizures meant letting his parents know he was sick, so they could be there to give him medicine in a timely fashion, and to be there to care for him while he was having a seizure.

"I'm sorry, Mom," Dylan apologized just as the phone rang.

"Hold that thought," his mother said as she got

up to answer the phone. "Hello?" His mom listened for a moment and then said, "Sure, absolutely, I'll be there." She hung up the phone with a groan. She ran a hand through her wavy, brown hair.

"Dylan," she smiled apologetically, "I'm needed at the hospital. A school bus was rear-ended by a truck at the 401 and Leslie, and several children were injured."

"Will the kids be okay?" asked Dylan.

"Yup, there are a lot of minor injuries, bumps, scrapes, bruises, and a lot of scared kids who need reassurance," replied his mother, picking her phone up off the counter. "I'm texting your dad now. He and Lucas should be back any minute."

Lucas and David returned from the walk a minute later and moments after that, Dylan's mom hurried off in the station wagon to the hospital, pausing just long enough to tell Dylan's dad when Dylan was next due for a dose of Advil.

Dylan spent the rest of the day in his room, either snoozing or working out the details of his plan to catch the peanut butter suspect. The conversation he had with his mother faded from his memory as he wrote out his ideas in his detective notebook.

Dylan decided that 'Operation Peanut Butter Suspect' would be divided into two plans, and he was debating whether to write each plan in a separate notebook when his dad knocked on his door. "Dylan,

Ethan's on the phone for you."

Dylan looked over at his clock, startled. It was 4:30 in the afternoon already!

He picked up the portable on his desk. "Hi, Ethan. How was school? Did Mrs. Cane give you guys a test?"

"Yup, spelling," replied Ethan. He didn't wait for Dylan to answer. "Are you okay? Your mom said you had a seizure."

"I'm okay," Dylan replied. "I hit my head pretty hard, though, when I was having it."

"Ouch," commiserated Ethan. "That must have hurt. You coming to school tomorrow? It was really boring without you."

"No," answered Dylan. "I've still got a fever, so I'm taking a bunch of Advil to keep my temperature down. Mom says I have to stay home at least one more day 'til the fever's gone."

"That sucks," said Ethan. "What did you do all day?"

Dylan stood up from the bed where he had been lounging and closed the door to his room. He lowered his voice to a loud whisper. "I'm writing out our Friday plan in two notebooks *and* I'm writing it in code in case the notebooks fall into the wrong hands."

"Good idea," agreed Ethan. "If your notes get found, nobody'll be able to understand what all the numbers mean. So, what's the first part of the plan?"

Dylan pulled open his desk drawer where he kept the paper with the decryption key of their alphabet-number code. He pulled it out from under several sheets of construction paper where he had it hidden. He lowered his voice even further and glancing at the sheet to make sure he had it right, he whispered the number sequence that meant 'phone' to Ethan. "16-8-15-14-5."

"Okay, so what's plan B?" whispered Ethan.

Again, Dylan listed the numbers from their code that meant 'park.' "16-1-18-11."

Ethan gave a low whistle. "Wow, so we're really doing this?"

"Yup," answered Dylan. "Gotta go; Dad'll be checking on me any minute."

"'Kay. Later," said Ethan.

Dylan hung up the phone. He picked up the notebook with the phone plan and reread it. He frowned. A niggling thought about using the phone to take photos was dancing around in his mind. If he could just put his finger on it...

Dylan's dad knocked on his door. "Time for dinner," he said, and the elusive thought about the camera on the phone dissipated.

The next morning Dylan's dad woke him, saying that Mom had come home really late last night and they were going to spend the morning on a walk to keep the noise level down so she could sleep in.

"We're taking a roundabout way," explained Dylan's dad as they set out after breakfast. "I don't want to go anywhere near the park. Lucas will most certainly want to play there if he thinks that's where we're headed."

Dylan nodded solemnly, acknowledging his dad's words. He was grinning on the inside though. This was a perfect chance to get some more information about the bad guys!

"Who do you think would do something like that to a kid's park?" asked Dylan. "Have they wrecked anything else at the park?"

Dylan's dad sighed loudly. "Unfortunately, yes, there has been more damage at the park. Mrs. Fitz, who walks her dogs there, told me yesterday that the brick walls of the washroom building were covered in graffiti. Next to a bunch of rude words and other nonsense, they also spray painted a name. Whoever it is, they're calling themselves the 'double SC.'" Dylan's dad shook his head. "I'd been thinking that the vandals are probably arrogant, ignorant teens with nothing better to do and it's looking more like it all the time."

Dylan's heart was thumping triple time now. His dad thought the bad guys were teenagers! They were probably the same students at Hailey's high school he had overheard the other night! It was just too bad he hadn't been able to catch a glimpse of them then.

"What does the 'SC' stand for, Dad?" asked Dylan. He didn't think his dad would know, but it was worth a shot.

"Mrs. Fitz didn't take the time to read the graffiti. As soon she saw the walls had been spray painted, she left the park immediately to phone it in to the non-emergency police number."

Dylan could hardly wait until tomorrow. Maybe the bad guys had also spray painted what SC stood for! The first thing he was going to do when he and Ethan got to the park, would be to read what was spray painted on the washroom building.

Lucas and his dad had been collecting colourful autumn leaves in a large, clear baggie on their walk. Dylan spotted one he thought would be perfect for the collection and was stooping to pick it up when he was jostled so hard, he dropped the leaf collection.

"Hey!" shouted his dad angrily. "Watch where you're going!"

Dylan stood up quickly, still clutching the red maple leaf in his hand, and looked around. He saw a guy on a skateboard zooming away. Hadn't he overheard one of the teens in the school hallway talking about being on a skateboard?

"Jerk," huffed his dad irately. He turned to Dylan. "You okay?"

"Yeah," answered Dylan, trying to peer past his dad to get a better look at the guy. He was already so far away that Dylan couldn't be sure what colour hair he had, or what he was wearing. Dylan felt frustrated. He was so close and yet so far from solving the mystery. Again!

"Let's head back," said Dylan's dad. "Lucas can play outside on the swing set before lunch."

"Sure," agreed Dylan quickly. He wanted to go home and write notes on what his dad had said about the latest vandalism at the park and about his brief run-in with 'skateboard guy.'

But Lucas didn't want any part of the plan to turn around and head home. When Dylan's dad turned to him, signing, "Home now," Lucas planted his feet firmly on the sidewalk and shook his head vehemently.

"Try signing swing set to him," advised Dylan as he knelt to pick up the leaves he had dropped.

"Good plan," replied Dylan's dad, and making sure he had eye contact with Lucas, he signed, "Let's go home and swing in the backyard."

As he was stuffing his leaf collection back into the bag he noticed a leaf on the edge of the sidewalk that looked different than the others. He reached for it and when he got a closer look at it, he saw it wasn't a leaf at all. It was some kind of a card. Dylan picked it up. It was a glossy business card. Dylan turned it over and read it, noting the card wasn't dirty at all and was just sitting on top of some leaves. It had probably been dropped recently. Dylan's heart stopped as he thought that, maybe, when he had brushed up against him, it was skateboarding guy who had dropped the card!

Deals for you: We Buy and Sell
111 Church St.
416 555 5555
Toronto

"Do you have your leaves picked up, Dylan?" asked Dylan's dad. Dylan looked up at the sound of his father's voice. Lucas was tugging on their father's hand, urging him to start walking.

"As you can see, Lucas loves your idea of playing in the backyard," chuckled Dylan's dad, affectionately tousling Lucas' hair. "He's in a major hurry, so let's get a move on."

Dylan carefully tucked the card in his plastic bag with the leaves, trying not to touch it any more than necessary. It could be evidence! Maybe it even had the skateboarder's fingerprints on it!

As he followed his dad and his brother home, he mused about the card he had found. Suddenly, he remembered that skateboard guy had been talking with his friend about looking for a place to sell the silverware set. That card was from a pawn shop, and it could prove skateboard guy was *also* the guy vandalizing the park!

CHAPTER TEN

D ylan ushered Ethan into his room and shut the door. It was Friday afternoon and the boys had just arrived home from school. Dylan felt much better. His throat wasn't sore anymore and he no longer had a fever.

"Tell me already!" urged Ethan. "You've been teasing me all day with this big secret of yours."

Dylan grinned. He had told Ethan all about the conversation he overheard at Hailey's school and about the graffiti with the mysterious 'SC' signature the vandals left, but had wanted to save his best news for now, when he could show it to his friend.

Dylan opened his closet door, reached into the very back, and pulled out the business card. When they had gotten home from the walk yesterday, he had carefully transferred the card from the leaf bag to a small Ziploc bag, being careful to handle the card only by its edges. He knew he had probably gotten his own fingerprints on the card when he initially handled it and he didn't want to add any more of his own prints to it. He handed the bag to Ethan with a flourish.

"Here it is, *proof* that skateboard guy is the bad guy wrecking the park."

Ethan took the bag from Dylan. He studied the card for a long time.

"Do you think we can dust it for fingerprints like they did in those mystery books you were showing me?" Dylan asked eagerly.

"Sure," replied Ethan slowly. "You've got flour, right?"

"Yeah, in the kitchen," said Dylan as he started opening his bedroom door.

"Wait," said Ethan. "We can probably get fingerprints from the card but we're going to need other prints to compare them to, to see if they match. And, your prints will probably be on it since you picked it up."

Dylan sank into his desk chair. "Oh, I didn't think of matching the fingerprints." The room grew quiet as the boys thought about the dilemma.

Ethan was the first to speak. "We should probably leave your door open so we can see when Hailey goes to the washroom."

"Right, I almost forgot." Dylan opened his door. "We're gonna have to talk quietly so my dad and Hailey don't hear any of our plans," he cautioned Ethan. Dylan sat at his desk and flipped randomly through his notebooks. "What about this? We can't match the bad guy's prints to anything else right now, but we can match mine."

Ethan's blue eyes widened in excitement. "Yes, fantastic! We'll fingerprint you and then we'll dust for prints on the card and match them up. The ones that don't match will be the bad guy's and we'll make sure to label them, so we don't get mixed up."

"Okay, so as soon as we get back from the park, we'll do the fingerprinting," said Dylan, looking out into the hallway through his open door. "We should figure out which bird song we want to use as our signal."

"Yeah," agreed Ethan. "It should be something simple that will stand out to you when you hear it."

"I heard a bird call the other morning," replied Dylan. "It was short, just two notes: one high, then low."

"Can you whistle it?" asked Ethan.

"I'll try." Dylan wet his lips and whistled the bird sound he had heard.

"Hey, that sounds easy," said Ethan. "I can do that." He gave an experimental whistle.

"Great," said Dylan. "Just make sure you do it really, really loudly in case there's trouble."

"No problem," assured Ethan, glancing in the direction of Dylan's open door. "Is your sister *ever* going to use the bathroom?"

"Maybe she went while I was showing you the card and we missed our chance," worried Dylan.

"I'm sure she'll go soon. We could always go to her room, look at her, then ask her what's on her face. She'll run to the bathroom to look at herself," giggled Ethan. "Aren't girls always worried about how they look?"

"Yeah," chortled Dylan. "On Wednesday, she was putting cream all over some huge pimple on her face."

The boys laughed.

"So ... do you wanna go get the flour so we're ready for later?" asked Ethan. "If Hailey leaves her room, I'll just dash in there and swipe her phone."

"Okay," replied Dylan, his brow furrowed as he thought about the best way to get the flour from the kitchen without attracting his father's attention.

"It's okay if you don't wanna get the flour now," said Ethan, noticing his best friend's frown.

"Yeah, I was just thinking what to say if my dad notices me getting the flour and asks me what I'm using it for," despaired Dylan.

"Well," suggested Ethan thoughtfully, "you could tell him we're experimenting with fingerprinting and promise we'll clean up our mess. You don't have to tell him why."

Dylan nodded. "True. Okay, I'll get some flour. We just need a bit, right? Like enough to fill half a mug?"

"That'll be enough," answered Ethan.

"Cool." Dylan threw his friend a weak grin and headed out the door to the kitchen. His heart was hammering wildly in his chest and it felt like his insides were twisted up like a pretzel. He didn't like all this sneaking around and having to be ready with half-truths to cover his actions.

Dylan was sliding quietly past his father, who was seated at the dining room table typing on his computer, when his dad looked up. "Hey, Mr. Pickle, you looking for a snack for you and Ethan?"

Dylan immediately bristled and his worry about having to explain why he was getting flour out of the kitchen was replaced with annoyance. His mom and dad hadn't called him 'Mr. Pickle' since grade one! It had been cute then, but now the nickname made him feel like a toddler.

Dylan stuffed his hands in his pocket and counted to ten. It was a technique his mom had taught Hailey to help her stop and think before saying something in anger she might regret. By the time Dylan got to ten, he realized his dad had given him the perfect cover for taking flour out of the kitchen.

"Yeah, we just have the munchies," answered Dylan. "Don't worry, we won't eat too much, we want to save room for dinner. It's spaghetti, right?"

"Yes, but it won't be for a while yet. Your mom's on a later shift today," answered his dad.

Dylan hurried into the kitchen and put some cookies on a plate. He glanced toward his dad. He saw his dad had the Google search browser open and was copying some notes from the screen on to paper. Okay. So far, so good. As Dylan poured some flour into a mug, he thought about how close they were to figuring out who the bad guy was. He could hardly wait to see the looks of admiration and respect on his parents' and Hailey's faces when the bad guys were caught, and all because of proof he and Ethan had found and collected.

Dylan hurried back to his room where Ethan was thumbing through his notebooks. "Your plans are awesome," his best friend enthused.

"Thanks," said Dylan, setting the plate of cookies and the mug with the flour down on his desk. "I also brought us a snack."

"I love Oreos," said Ethan as he took one. "Hailey's still in her room. She's talking on the phone, I think," he added, twisting the cookie apart and licking the frosting in the middle.

"We're going to run out of time!" Dylan was starting to despair when Hailey emerged from her room.

She stopped at Dylan's door. "Hey, I didn't know we had Oreos in the house." She glanced at the boys. "You left me some, right?"

"Yup," replied Dylan. He was about to tell her they were on the middle shelf in the baking cupboard when she turned and headed into the kitchen.

"Now's your chance," hissed Ethan. "Go!"

Dylan sprinted out of his room and dashed into his sister's. He headed for her desk where she always kept her phone, but it wasn't there! He quickly checked under her desk. Not there. He raced over to her nightstand. Not there either. She would be back any second! Where would her phone be? Maybe on her bed? It was a rumpled mess, though! He was starting to straighten her covers to see if the phone was somewhere on her bed, when he thought of her window seat. She spent a lot of time at her window, reading. He glanced over and there it was! He leaped around the bed, grabbed the phone, and hastily started to tuck it into his back pocket.

"What are you doing in my room?"

Dylan looked up in horror to see that his sister was in the doorway, looking right at him. Oh no! He was caught!

CHAPTER ELEVEN

Dylan stared at his sister for a long moment. He felt himself getting red in the face.

"You okay?" she asked, wiping cookie crumbs from her mouth.

Dylan slowly pushed her phone further into his pocket as he frantically thought about how to answer his sister. Could he say he was looking for his flashlight? His Legos? His *Planes* book? His sister would see right through those excuses! He hadn't played in her room in a while, so there would be no Lego bricks lying around. He and Hailey used to sit together and read on her window ledge, but they hadn't done that since the beginning of summer, so there wouldn't be any book left behind either. When he and Ethan were together they were never far from their flashlights and Hailey knew that.

Suddenly Hailey stepped forward, frowning as she looked at him. "You still got that fever?" she asked, touching his forehead.

Dylan felt his heart squeeze. He sucked in air, but it didn't feel like it was getting to his lungs. He felt short of breath, just like Hailey did when she had an asthma attack. He had never given much thought to what Hailey was experiencing during an asthma attack; she just took two puffs of her blue inhaler and got better. But if this was what it was like, it was awful! A surge of renewed respect went through him for his older sister. She was always so brave and matter of fact during an asthma attack.

He gulped. Finally, she was paying attention to him! She hadn't looked at him properly in weeks and weeks. and now, at the worst possible moment, he had the overprotective sister he knew and loved back, if only for a minute. She wore a look of concern and he leaned into the touch of her cool fingers brushing against his forehead. He wanted to stay with her there, forever, and the thought of breaking contact with her made his stomach twist. But the plan was in motion and being caught with her phone would wreck everything.

"I'm okay," he sputtered, reminding himself this would all be worth it once he and Ethan collected the evidence they needed to catch the bad guys. Hailey would be proud of him and want to spend quality time with him again. "I was looking for an extra pillow for tonight, but then I remembered you don't have one." He edged past her, keeping his backside toward the door frame and away from her view.

Hailey shrugged. "You're acting weirder than usual, Thing One," she said, closing her door behind him.

"What took you so long?" asked Ethan, impatiently pushing his long hair away from his forehead.

"Hailey caught me and I had to make something up quick." Dylan shut the door to his room. "I got it!" He hurriedly flashed the phone at Ethan before stashing it back in his pocket.

"Let's go!" urged Ethan.

The boys headed into the living room where Dylan's dad was writing. Lucas was under the dining room table, contentedly lining up his trains.

"Hey, Dad," began Dylan hesitantly. "Ethan dropped something out of his backpack on the way home from school. Is it okay if we go out to look for it?"

Dylan's dad glanced briefly in the boys' direction. "Sure," he said, frowning as he returned his gaze to the laptop. "I need a better word," he muttered and reached for his thesaurus as the boys left the house.

Once outside, the friends high-fived each other. "Yes, that was easy," crowed Ethan happily.

Too easy, thought Dylan with chagrin as they started along the sidewalk. His dad had hardly even looked at them! He probably hadn't heard what they were saying, either.

Ethan tugged at Dylan's sleeve. "We gotta stop at my house. We need bags to collect the evidence in and gloves to wear. We don't want to contaminate anything we find with our own fingerprints."

"Oh, yeah, true," replied Dylan, wishing, not for the first time, he was half as smart as Ethan. He followed him up the walkway and waited while Ethan fished a key out of his pocket. Ethan's mom was a veterinarian and stayed late at the clinic on the Fridays Ethan slept over at Dylan's.

Ethan unlocked his front door and they stepped into the house. After collecting Ziploc bags and thin latex gloves, the boys headed back out toward the park.

Dylan's heart was starting to beat faster and his stomach was in knots. He turned to Ethan. "How about we practice the bird call, so we know what to do just in case."

"Good idea," replied Ethan, making the bird call sound. It was easy, and after each making the call twice, the boys fell silent as they continued their walk to the park.

Dylan had hoped practicing the bird call would distract him from his racing thoughts and rapidly thumping heart, but he couldn't stop imagining what would happen when they got to the park. Would there be more vandalism? Would there be any evidence to collect? Would the bad guys be there?

When they got in view of the park, Ethan stopped and handed Dylan the gloves and bags. "Okay, so I'll wait at the edge of the parking lot where I can see anybody coming from all directions." He tucked his long, wavy locks behind his ear.

"You need a haircut," teased Dylan, slipping on

the gloves.

"Nope," answered Ethan. "I'm growing it out to give to this place that makes wigs for people with cancer to wear."

"That's cool," replied Dylan. "Since when were you gonna do that?"

"Since last week," grinned Ethan. "I forgot to tell you. I saw a post on my mom's Facebook wall about it."

Dylan smiled and touched his own shaggy hair. "Maybe I should do that too," he mused.

"Yeah, your hair is getting pretty long," said Ethan. He rubbed his hands together. "You ready for operation park?"

"Yeah, *so* ready," answered Dylan as he pulled Hailey's phone out of his pocket.

Dylan and Ethan proceeded briskly into the park. Ethan stopped at one edge of the parking lot and gave a thumbs-up to Dylan. Dylan paused a moment and looked around the park. Usually it was full of kids playing on the climber, running around, jumping off the swings, playing in the sand. Now it was quiet in the abandoned park. Dylan gulped in air. It felt like the silence was everywhere, smothering him. It was eerie to not hear kids laughing, happily calling to one another, and to not hear the low undertones of adults chatting with one another as they kept a watchful eye on their children.

Dylan headed over to the brown brick building

that housed the men's and women's restrooms with a renewed sense of purpose. If he could get some really good proof today, not only would it benefit Dylan, but it would help all the kids in the neighbourhood get their beloved park back.

First, he wanted to get a closer look at the graffiti. Maybe he could figure out what 'SC' stood for. He took a moment to find the camera app on the phone. Hailey had let him play around on her phone after she had first gotten it, so he knew the key to unlocking her phone was to swipe a specific pattern on the screen. He hoped fervently she was still using the small 'h' outline. His right hand trembled as he carefully traced the letter 'h' on the grid of dots on her phone.

He exhaled with relief when the unlock tones chimed and he quickly tapped on the camera app.

Dylan walked around the whole building and saw there was only graffiti on the wall facing the parking lot, next to the large, sparsely treed, grassy area. He stopped near the wall to study the graffiti. The letters 'SC' were encircled by a double ring in the centre of the wall, surrounded by all sorts of weird symbols and squiggles. He stepped even closer to inspect the markings and as he looked down, he saw what looked like groups of letters in the bottom right corner. He knelt to inspect them. His heart thumped hard and fast as he read what was written: Scarborough Scarers.

Dylan quickly opened the camera app, focused, and snapped a photo of the words. He couldn't believe the bad guys were bold enough to write their name! Dylan straightened and stepped back to take a picture of the other graffiti.

Dylan glanced toward the playground equipment. Would he see peanut butter smeared on railings? Would there be dog poop or broken glass? He started toward the climber with the three slides. As he stepped off the concrete floor by the restrooms and onto the sand by the climber, he felt something crack under his foot. He crouched down and saw the black lid of a spray paint can, half squashed into the sand. He pulled a bag out of his front jeans pocket and carefully dropped the lid into it.

Dylan slowly walked around the climber as he examined it for signs of vandalism, Hailey's phone in his hand, ready to take photos. Suddenly her phone vibrated and then rang. He jumped and dropped it. He picked it up and almost let it slip out of his hand again when he saw the display on her screen: *Home calling.* Oh no! What was he going to do now?

CHAPTER TWELVE

D ylan thought his heart was going to beat right out of his chest. He stood frozen for several long seconds, gripping the phone tightly. By the third ring, he knew what to do. He hit the ignore button to disconnect the call and turned the phone off.

Dylan ran over to Ethan. "We have a *huge* problem!" he panted, trying to catch his breath from his mad dash across the park.

"What?" asked Ethan worriedly as he looked around the park. "Were we spotted?"

"No, Hailey's phone just rang. She called from our home line. It's what she does when she can't find the phone in the house," explained Dylan. "She follows the sound of the ringing 'til she finds it."

Ethan looked grave. "Oh, this is bad. This is very, very bad. What did you do?"

"I hit ignore and turned it off," answered Dylan.

"Okay, damage control," proclaimed Ethan solemnly. "She's looking for her phone, but she doesn't know we have it. We need to sneak it back into her room and when she finds it, we'll play dumb and act like we don't know anything about it."

Dylan nodded and then groaned as that elusive thought about using the phone to take pictures came to him. Ethan would actually have to play dumb, but

Dylan wouldn't! He groaned again as he thought about all the time he'd put into the phone plan, forgetting the one huge issue that could mess everything up.

"I just thought of something else," he said as he turned Hailey's phone on again. "When Hailey has her phone back, she'll see the photos we took! We have to delete them off her phone, otherwise our whole plan is ruined. She'll see what we've been doing and tell Mom and Dad!"

Ethan interrupted Dylan's fretting. "Don't forget to delete the photos from her 'recently deleted' file too!" he urged in a panicked voice. "Good thing you thought of getting rid of them!"

After deleting the photos and turning off the phone, the boys hurried out of the park.

"Well, that was a waste of time," said Dylan despondently, taking off the gloves and putting them in his pocket. "We can't even use the photos for evidence now."

"Yeah, but you only took two and we could probably sketch out what you saw when we get to your house," consoled Ethan.

Dylan brightened. "True," he agreed, suddenly remembering the bag of evidence he was still clutching. "*And* I found this," he continued, showing the bag with the paint can lid to Ethan.

"Cool!" exclaimed Ethan. "Right after supper we'll..."

Dylan was opening his mouth to ask why Ethan had so abruptly stopped speaking when he saw Hailey approaching them. Oh no! Could this day get any worse? Dylan exchanged a quick glance with Ethan and put his hand with the evidence behind his back.

"I've got this," mumbled Ethan, putting on a huge, fake smile. "What's up?" he asked Hailey in a loud, carefree voice once she had caught up to them.

"What's up? I'll tell you what's up!" huffed Hailey with annoyance. "Dad's wondering where you guys are. You were supposed to be back, like, half an hour ago, and he's starting to get angry and worried. And now, instead of being able to finish my homework, he's got me scouring the neighbourhood for you two!"

Ethan shrugged. "Sorry, I guess we just lost track of time."

"Hmmph," said Hailey as she turned to head toward home. The boys had only taken a few steps when she turned around and looked at Dylan. "Did you see my phone when you were in my room this afternoon?"

Dylan swallowed hard and told the biggest lie he had ever told. "Nope," he said. "Are you missing it?"

"Duh, I wouldn't be asking you about it if I knew where it was," replied Hailey snarkily. She headed along the sidewalk ahead of the boys at a brisk pace.

"Phew, that was close," said Ethan in an undertone once Hailey was out of earshot.

98

"Yeah," replied Dylan.

Dylan's dad was waiting for them when they got in the front door. "Where have you *been*?" he asked, his voice terse as he ran a hand through his short, dark hair. "I was starting to worry."

"Sorry, Dad," apologized Dylan quickly. Dylan's dad was usually calm and even-tempered, and it made Dylan's stomach do jumping jacks to see his father angry with him. "It took us longer than we thought," he added, his voice trailing off into a mumble. He told himself he wasn't technically lying to his dad by using the vague word 'it.' He was still telling part of the truth. He just wasn't explaining what the 'it' really meant.

"Well, you're back safe and sound and that's all that matters," said Dylan's dad after a long moment of studying the boys. "Dinner'll be ready in half an hour." He headed into the kitchen.

"Do you think your dad believed us?" asked Ethan once the friends were established in Dylan's room, and Dylan had put the bag with the paint can lid in his desk drawer.

"I don't know," replied Dylan, sighing heavily. He hated being dishonest and sneaky. It felt like his stomach had been one huge knot all afternoon. And they still had to sneak the phone back into Hailey's room!

Dylan sprawled out on his back on his bed. "When Dad calls us for supper, we'll wait 'til Hailey goes first, then I'll toss the phone back in her room. I'm gonna put it under her blankets on her bed. Her bed's so messy, she'll just think it was hidden under the covers this whole time."

"Sounds good," said Ethan. "Let's get everything ready to do the fingerprinting."

Dylan and Ethan had cleared off Dylan's desk to make room for their detective work when Dylan's mom rapped lightly on his open door. "Hi, guys. Spaghetti's ready."

"Hi, Mom," smiled Dylan as he pulled her in for a hug. She had changed out of her work uniform and was wearing her favourite gray sweatpants and a light blue T-shirt. Dylan breathed in deeply, savouring the scent of vanilla she always wore.

"Hi, Mrs. Marcotte," said Ethan, as Dylan stepped back from embracing his mother. "We'll be at the table in a minute," he said, throwing Dylan a brief, but meaningful look. "We just have to wash our hands."

"No problem, boys," replied Dylan's mom as she headed down the hall to let Hailey know it was suppertime.

"It'll only take a second for you to put her phone back," said Ethan, grinning at Dylan. "Easy peasy, lemon squeezy," he rhymed, waggling his eyebrows.

Dylan laughed and high-fived Ethan. He was thankful to have such an easygoing, fun-loving best friend. With his best buddy by his side, everything felt right and even if things weren't working out as planned, Ethan could always be counted on to uncomplainingly come up with a solution.

Returning the phone to Hailey's room was as easy as Ethan had predicted. As soon as Dylan saw her walk down the hall toward the kitchen, he sprinted into her room and hastily jammed the phone under her covers near the foot of her bed.

"You'll find it," Dylan's mom was reassuring Hailey when the boys entered the kitchen for supper. "It can't be far, after all, it's pretty much surgically attached to you most days," joked their mother, trying to lighten the mood. "And since you've been pretty good about keeping your room neat, it should be easy to find in there."

Alexandra turned to David, wagging her finger at him sternly. "Now, had she lost the phone in the garage, it'd be gone forever. David, please, let's at least get a start on decluttering the garage so we can finally get to the door and get it rolling up and down again. I'd *really* like to get the car in there by the winter."

"You're right," agreed David. "I've been putting it off for too long." He clapped his hands together. "Okay, so Sunday morning I'll set the manuscript aside and we'll start on it."

Lucas picked up his plate and thrust it at Alexandra.

Dylan's mom laughed. "Okay, okay, some of us are very hungry," she smiled indulgently, taking Lucas's plate and starting to put spaghetti on it.

After dinner, Dylan and Ethan worked on getting a fingerprint from Dylan so they would have something to compare to any they found on the business card.

"We'll use your black binder," suggested Ethan. "It's got a shiny, plastic cover and we'll be able to see your print more clearly. Also, we'll use your thumb. It works better."

"How do you know all that?' asked Dylan.

"Last week when I was putting all my books back on the shelves, I decided to try some of the fingerprinting techniques to see if they actually worked," answered Ethan.

"Okay, so what do I have to do?" asked Dylan.

"First you have to dip your thumb in the flour to cover it. Then all you have to do is press your thumb on to the binder. We'll probably have to do it a few times 'til we get a clear print."

Dylan obligingly coated the pad of his thumb with flour and pressed it firmly onto his binder. "Hey, it worked!" he exclaimed. He frowned as he leaned in to examine the print. "It's not very clear, though."

"Get out your magnifying class," said Ethan. "That'll help. Oh, and do some more prints. You probably had too much flour on your thumb."

It was not until the fourth print, with Dylan

inspecting them through the magnifying glass, that he could start to see a distinct pattern of lines and swirls from his thumb.

"Let's do the lid now and then the card," Dylan said, excited now that the fingerprinting seemed to be working.

"It's going to be a bit different doing the lid and the card," cautioned Ethan. "We're not making prints; we're going to have to dust for them really carefully so we don't smudge anything that might be there."

Dylan nodded and opened his closet door to get the business card he had hidden. His hands shook and they felt clammy with sweat. He was nervous. This was important work and making even one mistake could ruin everything.

"How about you do the actual dusting?" he suggested to Ethan. "You've already practiced fingerprinting," he continued. "I don't wanna mess stuff up," he said, his voice trailing off uncertainly.

"Okay," replied Ethan slowly, as he glanced at Dylan. "You're really good at being a detective, you know. You notice things most other people don't and you make good notes about it. And besides, we wouldn't even have anything to fingerprint if it weren't for you."

Dylan managed a small smile in acknowledgement of Ethan's comments and opened his desk drawer to take out the paint can lid. He wasn't sure how to respond to Ethan. He was sure his best friend was only saying those things because he was too polite to agree that they were actually better off with the more capable friend doing the important detective work.

Ethan carefully opened the bag with the card. He tipped the bag so that the card slid out of it onto Dylan's desk. "See, no hands," joked Ethan.

Next, he took some flour out of the mug and held it between his palms. Holding his hands over the card, he rubbed them together and a light sprinkling of flour floated down to coat the card. "It doesn't clump so much when I do it this way," explained Ethan.

"Okay, cross your fingers," said Ethan. "I'm going to blow off the extra flour and we'll see if there are any prints. Be ready with your magnifying glass." Ethan bent close to the card and gently blew off the extra flour.

"I think I see something!" said Dylan excitedly as he picked up his magnifying glass. He leaned in and studied the card. "That guy sure has a big thumb," he stated, handing the magnifying glass to Ethan. "Look."

"Yup," agreed Ethan. "It's a pretty good print. Let's do the lid now."

Dylan carefully opened the bag with the paint can lid. Emboldened by their success with the card, he copied Ethan's technique and tipped the lid slowly out of the baggie on to his desk.

"This is going to be tricky," warned Ethan. "It's going to be awkward dusting it and keeping it from rolling around."

Dylan looked around his room while he thought. "Hey, how about we put it in my Kleenex box? I used a lot of tissues when I was sick, so it's almost empty. The box will keep the lid from rolling off the desk onto the floor."

"Excellent!" said Ethan, taking the Kleenex box off Dylan's nightstand. He quickly pulled out the remaining tissues, set them aside, and widened the opening of the box by tearing off the cardboard around the narrow opening.

"Ta da," Ethan said triumphantly, holding the box up. "We are ready for phase two."

Using the baggie, Ethan guided the paint can lid off the desk and into the box. He dusted the lid carefully, repeating the procedure he'd used with the card.

"You guys want a snack?" came Dylan's mom's voice at the door as the boys were closely examining the lid to see if any fingerprints had been revealed.

Dylan and Ethan both startled and as they turned toward Dylan's mom, they jostled the box and it fell on the floor!

"Uh, no thanks, we're okay," stammered Dylan. They needed to get her out of his room quickly, without attracting her suspicion. Once she started asking questions he knew he wouldn't be able to keep lying to her. He shuffled his feet and stuffed his hands in his pocket to keep them from shaking.

"You guys have been very quiet," noted Alexandra, stepping further into the room. "What have you been up to?"

"Not much," replied Ethan, casually adjusting his position so he was standing in front of where the box had fallen, shielding it from Alexandra's view.

"Actually, Mom," blurted out Dylan. "A snack would be good. I've just been thinking about how hungry I am."

Dylan's mother tucked her hair behind her ear and frowned questioningly. "Did you not eat enough dinner?"

Dylan suppressed a huge groan. He shouldn't have said anything at all! Now he was just making things worse!

"Dylan meant he's so hungry for a snack," explained Ethan, rescuing his best friend. "We had lots of pasta, but we're in the mood for something sweet."

"Okay, I think there are cookies left. Do you want milk too?" asked Dylan's mother, her confused, questioning look disappearing, to be replaced with a smile.

"Yes, please," replied Dylan, relieved.

"I'll set it out for you in the kitchen then, for when you're ready," said Dylan's mother as she left his room.

"Thanks!" called out Ethan to Dylan's mom as he knelt to carefully pick up the box. "The lid rolled out of it, but I think it's okay. Hand me the baggie; I just have to push the lid back in," he instructed. Dylan held his breath as he watched his best friend carefully manoeuvre the lid into the box and the box back onto the desk.

"Let's get our snack, then check out if there are fingerprints on the lid," suggested Dylan with a massive sigh of relief once the box and lid were safely back in place on his desk.

After downing four cookies and two glasses of milk each, the boys returned to Dylan's room to examine the paint can lid for prints.

"It's smudged, but it's a big smudge and it sorta looks like the print on the card," said Ethan after studying the print closely with the magnifying glass.

"What do you think? Do they match?" asked Dylan hopefully.

"Maybe," said Ethan softly. "But maybe not."

Dylan sank onto his bed, tears pricking his eyes. They'd done so much work! They'd avoided being caught several times. They'd successfully figured out solutions to all sorts of little problems they'd run into over the course of the afternoon and evening. Now, after everything, they were no further ahead. All they had was a lousy business card and a junky old paint can lid, and no proof showing skateboard guy was doing the vandalism at the park, and still no idea who the bad guy in the neighbourhood was.

Dylan flopped back on his bed, despondent. It was time to give up being a detective. He looked over at Ethan. "Let's just forget the whole thing. I'm done. It's over."

"Aw, come on, Dyl. Don't give up. We'll find more evidence," pleaded Ethan.

Dylan wiped away stray tears trickling down his cheeks he hadn't managed to hold back. He shrugged. "It's okay. I don't wanna do this anymore." He rubbed his stomach. "Now at least my belly's not going to feel all tied up in knots anymore."

Ethan took a tissue off Dylan's nightstand and started wiping off Dylan's desk. "Okay," he conceded slowly. "We may as well clean up. Whoa, that flour got everywhere."

The boys cleaned in silence for several minutes before Dylan spoke. "Did you bring your Morse code book? We could practice that," he suggested.

Ethan paused in wiping flour off the portable phone. "Yeah," he grinned. "I did. I never took it out of my backpack."

CHAPTER THIRTEEN

The following Sunday morning, Dylan woke up early. He sat up in bed and draped his covers around him. He felt warm and cozy and best of all, his stomach didn't hurt—not even a little bit. He smiled as he idly tapped out SOS, the Morse code call for help Ethan had taught him Friday night. Ethan had explained that a lot of people thought SOS stood for *'save our souls,'* or *'save our ship,'* but the letters didn't actually stand for anything at all. They had been chosen simply because, taken together, they were very easy to send and had a distinct, unmistakeable sound. He tapped the code again. Three quick taps, then three slow taps, followed by three quick taps.

Dylan stretched and tucked the covers more securely under his feet. Learning Morse code had been much easier than he had thought and Ethan had made it fun.

"Good to see you're already awake, Mr. Pickle," said his mother, coming into his room and opening his drapes. "Did you sleep well?"

Dylan pushed his covers off and swung his feet around to the floor, frowning. He had been planning to talk with his parents during Meeting and Game Night yesterday about his worries they were still treating him like he was a little kid, and his concerns about how many more kids they were going to adopt, but his dad had gotten a call from his publisher during the meeting and been tied up on the phone. By the time the call was done, Lucas was starting to get impatient and they had skipped quickly to the last part of the meeting, the weekly schedule. After that, they'd played Dylan's favourite game, Charades. It had been so much fun and his Alexandra's attempts at acting out even the easiest words had Dylan and his family in stitches. By the time he'd gone to bed, thoughts of speaking with his parents had vanished.

"What's with the frown?" asked his mother.

"Nothing," replied Dylan, as he offered his mother a weak smile and a half-truth. "The garage is a huge mess. Are we going to have to clean it *all* day?" It was true, he hadn't been at all thrilled at the idea of spending his Sunday cleaning out the garage when his dad had told them about it at the meeting last night. If his parents weren't too busy, he promised himself, he'd speak with them tonight for sure.

"Not all day," answered his mother. "Just the morning. You don't need to dress too warmly. This Indian summer just won't quit. It's hot as blazes out there. Oh, I almost forgot; Ethan and his mom are coming over to help, so that'll make the job more fun," she placated Dylan. "Breakfast is in ten minutes," she said, leaving his room and heading to Hailey's.

"Are you *kidding* me?" asked Hailey

incredulously as she peered into the small, one car garage later that morning after a hearty breakfast of oatmeal, toast, and fruit. She stepped back in disgust after surveying the garage. Over the last few years, it had become the place the Marcotte family used to store items they no longer wanted in the house, or items that were broken but too big for weekly garbage collection, but not worth a trip to the dump. The only items readily accessible were the lawn mower and various snow shovels.

David had just unlocked the side door to the garage and now he stood back, a sheepish expression on his face. "I know, I know, it's bad." He turned to Ethan and his mom, who had come over after breakfast dressed in old sweatpants and T-shirts, ready to help declutter. "If you want to bail, I don't blame you."

"No, of course not," replied Ethan's mom. "Many hands make light work, isn't that how the saying goes?"

"More like a thousand hands, and a huge garbage truck," muttered Hailey beside Dylan.

Alexandra rubbed her hands together. "We'll start by taking out one thing at a time and sorting stuff into three piles: Keep. Donate. Toss." After showing everyone where each pile would be, the great garage clean-out, as Dylan had come to think of it, began.

Several hours later, Dylan was standing alone in the garage, holding a rake with one tine missing that

Hailey had thrust at him before going into the house to use the washroom. His parents and Ethan's mom had begun rolling used tires out of the garage and were at the garbage pile. It was hot, sweaty work decluttering, and Dylan wiped off his forehead with the sleeve of his shirt.

Ethan was keeping Lucas occupied at the swing set. Lucas had only been interested in helping clean the garage for the first ten minutes and after that, had become cranky and impatient. After David had stumbled into Lucas and almost knocked him over for the third time, it was decided everyone would get a 'break' from cleaning by taking turns keeping Lucas safely and happily amused playing in the backyard.

Not sure where his dad wanted an only slightly damaged rake, Dylan started to exit the garage. He stopped abruptly in the doorway when he heard what Ethan's mom was saying to his parents.

"...shielding Ethan from what's going on in the neighbourhood. It's bad enough there's some yahoo running around vandalizing the park, he doesn't need to know the rest of it."

"We've kept the information from Dylan and Hailey as well," he heard his mother reply.

"I ran into Mrs. Fitz at No Frills the other morning," he heard Ethan's mother begin before she lowered her voice considerably and Dylan had to strain to hear the rest of her comment. He could only hear every other word and he stepped forward as much as he dared, still clutching the rake.

"Mr. Malone … early from work … caught … guy in a hoodie … garage … broad daylight … chased him … with a baseball bat … police … station … smart thing … new lock … your…" The screen door slammed loudly, making Dylan jump.

"Public service announcement: I poured the last of the soap refill into the soap dispenser," said Hailey, coming out of the house and drying her hands on her jeans. "Just like you wanted—telling you *before* stuff runs out," she added with a 'so there' glance at her mother.

"Did you write it on the grocery list on the fridge?" asked Alexandra.

"No," huffed Hailey exasperatedly. "Fine, I guess I'll go do that too." She stomped back into the house mumbling about servants and wasting her Sunday.

Dylan hurriedly leaned the rake against the wall and raced over to Ethan. He couldn't wait to tell him what he had heard!

CHAPTER FOURTEEN

"The bad guy we're not supposed to know about got caught!" he announced dramatically.

Ethan pumped his legs one more time and jumped off the swing, arms outstretched, landing with a soft thud on the grass.

"What?"

"That looked like you were flying!" said Dylan, impressed.

"I know, right?" replied Ethan. "What were you saying about the bad guy?"

Dylan eagerly launched into the story he had overheard Ethan's mom telling his parents. "And after that, the bad guy got taken to the police station after Mr. Malone chased him down," he concluded.

"Is that all they said?" asked Ethan, settling Lucas on the swing after discretely putting down the pile of twigs Lucas had been collecting and had pressed into his hand. "Did they say anything about when we could go back to the park?"

"Dylan, it's not your break yet!" called Hailey with annoyance as she came over to the boys. "It's my turn to be on Thing Two duty. You guys can go back to cleaning out the horror story that is the garage."

The boys trudged back to the garage where Alexandra was standing, still talking with David and

Ethan's mom.

"...even if we could get that shelving unit moved that's jammed up against the garage door, there are still the rusted wheels and ball bearings in the door track to deal with." She sighed. "We'll probably need to call someone from that garage door place on Lawrence Ave."

"True," answered Dylan's dad. "Let's call it a day. We've accomplished quite a bit. We've actually got room to move around in the garage now. We'll just bag the donations and start loading the car. We'll finish this next Saturday," he concluded.

"I'll see you later then," said Ethan's mom. She turned to her son. "We've got time to make the 1:30 showing of *Miss Peregrine's Home for Peculiar Children*. I've got just enough Scene points now for both our admissions," she said with a grin as she and Ethan headed out of the backyard.

"Must be nice to see a movie," grumbled Hailey as she and Dylan began helping their dad load the car for the trip to the nearby second-hand store, Value Village.

Dylan fell into bed that night, exhausted from the day. He was determined to stay awake, though. Alexandra had been called to the hospital to cover part of a shift for a co-worker who had gotten sick and wasn't back yet. He and Hailey had spent the rest of the afternoon with their dad lugging donations to

Value Village and helping to install hooks in the garage to hang the shovels and gardening tools on, all the while keeping an eye on Lucas. Dylan lay awake as long as he could, waiting for his mother to return so he could finally talk with her and his dad about his worries, but it got later and later and Dylan's eyes got heavier and heavier, until finally they closed as sleep overtook him.

"Fine with me, you big know-it-all!" yelled Dylan angrily as he stomped up the steps to his front door on Monday after school.

"Fine!" shouted Ethan back, just as angrily, as he headed up the walkway to his house.

"Hey, what's your problem?" said Hailey, as Dylan crashed noisily through the front door.

Dylan kicked off his shoes and shrugged out of his jacket.

"Just mad," he mumbled, glancing around the living room. "Where's Dad?"

"I found this note on the kitchen table when I got home," she said, thrusting a piece of paper at Dylan. "Lucas fell off the swing and broke his wrists. Mom and Dad took him to the hospital."

All thoughts of his fight with Ethan flew out of Dylan's head as he took in Hailey's words. "Is Lucas gonna be okay?"

"Yeah, Mom's with him," answered Hailey,

heading to her room. "She's the best nurse around. She'll know exactly what to do."

When Dylan tried to follow Hailey to her room, she stopped him. "Dyl, I have homework," she said, busy readjusting the ponytail in her hair and not looking at him. "Everything's gonna be okay. Just play with your Legos or something. We'll have Kraft dinner later."

"But I just wanna..." began Dylan when Hailey's phone rang.

She pulled it out of her back pocket and glanced at the screen before answering the call. "Keisha! Oh my God! It's been, like, forever!"

Hailey waved Dylan off before going into her room and firmly shutting the door.

Dylan stood at her door for several minutes before slowly returning to his room. He swept aside the DVD of *The Lego Movie* he'd left lying on his bed and sank down on his covers. His heart had been beating hard and fast since hearing the news about Lucas, but now it was slowing down. He reached over to his nightstand, picked up his flashlight and twirled it around on his bed. Hailey seemed confident Lucas was going to be okay and that their mom would be able to fix him up good as new. He thought about calling Ethan, but then he remembered their fight. He was sure Ethan wouldn't want to talk to him, not after being called a know-it-all. Dylan wished with all his heart he could take back what he said.

Dylan thought of the popular song, "Everything is Awesome," from the movie he'd tossed onto the floor. Everything was *not* awesome, he thought grimly. Everything was awful. The day had started out okay, but by second nutrition break, Ethan's comments and questions had started to irritate Dylan. Ethan had asked him if he had spoken with his parents about his concerns and when Dylan had explained why he hadn't, Ethan's tone had turned judgemental. "Well, if it had been *me, I* would have stayed up," he'd stated loftily. "You can't keep putting stuff off."

Dylan sighed and rolled over. As if that wasn't bad enough, Ethan had commented several times that maybe Dylan hadn't heard everything, that he'd gotten the story wrong, that the bad guy was still on the loose. Ethan claimed his mom insisted the park was still off-limits because no one had been caught yet. When Dylan tried to explain that maybe there were two different bad guys in their neighbourhood, one doing the vandalizing and another guy breaking into garages and cars, Ethan had dismissed his ideas, saying they were wrong. He'd accused Dylan of contradicting himself. "First, you were so sure it was one guy and now you think it's two?" he'd snapped. "So make up your mind, which is it?"

It had been the last straw for Dylan when Ethan had started throwing around words like 'coincidental' and 'probability.' How was Dylan supposed to defend himself if he didn't even know what the words meant? Dylan had shouted at Ethan that he was just using big words to win the argument and Ethan had yelled back that he wasn't.

Dylan sat up abruptly. His stomach was starting to hurt. He picked up *The Lego Movie* off his floor and plodded into the living room. He hoped watching one of his favourite movies would take his mind off his fight with Ethan and his worries about Lucas.

He slid the DVD into the player, plunked himself on the couch and settled back to watch. The movie was at his favourite part, where the bad guys were fighting the master builders and Bat Man was saying some pretty funny things, when suddenly Dylan heard something that made his heart start to pound quickly again. It was a banging noise coming from their back door by the garage. Dylan turned off the movie, got off the couch and picked up the portable phone. His heart was beating like a jackhammer as he wondered who could be rattling around at their back door.

He headed to Hailey's room to ask her if she heard anything. He could hear her laughing. She was *still* on the phone! She was saying, "Remember that time at the Dunlops when we all..." when he turned away. She wouldn't want to be interrupted by him with talk of weird noises. Besides, it was probably nothing. All this talk about bad guys was making him imagine things. Nonetheless, he tiptoed cautiously down the hall in the direction of the back door, phone in hand.

He peeked out the window of the back door and what he saw made his insides turn to jelly. A guy in a gray hoodie was trying to bust open the lock on their garage door! He was using a long-handled tool to cut the lock off.

Dylan ducked down so he wouldn't be seen. He made several decisions all at once. As he tapped out 911 on the phone he realized this was his big chance to catch the bad guy. He thought fleetingly of signalling Ethan somehow and then exhaled loudly. There was no point. Ethan was probably still mad and would just ignore any message from Dylan.

Dylan took a deep breath, stood up, and was stealthily letting himself out of the house when he heard a voice on the phone. "911, what is your emergency?"

Dylan didn't take the time to answer. He knew exactly how he was going to trap the thief, but he needed to do it *now*. He tiptoed out the door and stepped gingerly over the tool the teen had left lying on the ground. Five steps later, he was at the door of the garage. He slammed it shut and pushed the bolt across, locking the guy in the garage. Suddenly, the enormity of what he had done sank in. A good detective *always* had a backup plan. He'd already called 911, but it couldn't hurt to send out another distress signal. The Morse code one he had learned from Ethan felt like it would take too long to whistle, but the bird call was only two notes. Dylan whistled the bird call loudly, piercingly, before putting the phone to his ear to speak with the 911 operator who was still on the line asking him to state his emergency.

Suddenly, the phone was roughly ripped out of his hand. Dylan's heart was beating right out of his chest as he looked up in horror. There was a second bad guy, staring right at him!

CHAPTER FIFTEEN

A tall teen with long, greasy blond hair was smiling malevolently at him.

"Look at the little boy, trying to be the hero," he snarled. The guy inside the garage was now yelling very bad words and banging repeatedly on the garage door trying to escape. The greasy haired teen threw the phone on the ground and stomped on it several times. He slammed hard into Dylan, sending him sprawling against the brick wall of the house beside the garage. Then the teen reached for the garage door to release his friend.

"Hey!" exclaimed Ethan from around the corner. "Hey!" he repeated, this time screaming at full volume.

The greasy haired teen turned around, startled, to see who had called out. It was all the distraction Dylan needed. He leapt to his feet, picked up the discarded lock-busting tool and giving it a powerful swing, bashed it onto the side of his attacker's head. The teen crumpled to the ground, unconscious.

"Oh my God, you knocked him out!" said Ethan, running to Dylan's side.

Dylan's legs suddenly gave out and he slumped down to sit on the grass.

From inside the garage there came bursts of muffled cursing, yelling, and banging as the teen trapped inside the Marcotte's garage discovered he couldn't lift the jammed garage door to escape.

"We've got to call 911!" urged Ethan, his eyes widening and panic flooding his voice upon hearing the commotion in the garage.

"I already did, just before the guy smashed my phone," replied Dylan, rubbing the back of his head. "I'm not sure it worked, though. I didn't get to say anything to the operator."

"We have to call again, then!" said Ethan. "Is Hailey here? We can use her phone."

"Yeah, she's inside," answered Dylan, his voice shaking. "Can you get her? My head hurts pretty bad," he moaned as Hailey came flying out the back door.

"What's going on? I heard banging and yelling..." Hailey stopped abruptly as she took in the scene in front of her. She knelt beside Dylan and started tapping on her phone. "I'm calling 911."

"I'm sorry I called you a know-it-all," groaned Dylan to Ethan. "I'm sorry I yelled. I don't want to fight."

"Me, neither," said Ethan as the sound of sirens filled the air and several firefighters burst into the backyard, preceded by Ethan's mom, repeating, "They're here, they're back here."

Everything happened quickly after that. The police arrived two minutes later while the firefighters were checking over Dylan and the unconscious youth.

Dylan's parents and Lucas arrived home from the hospital to see the thief being led down their driveway in handcuffs to the police cruiser. The thief's greasy haired accomplice was wheeled out of the backyard on a stretcher, a police officer accompanying him in the ambulance to the hospital.

EPILOGUE

Five days later...

It was Saturday after supper and Dylan was curled up in his favourite chair waiting for Ethan and his mom to arrive. They had been invited to join the Marcotte family Meeting and Game Night. He was rereading the front-page news article in the local newspaper, *The Scarborough Mirror,* chronicling the story of how he had caught the Scarborough Scarers.

He smiled as he ran his fingers over the headline: "Local Nine-year-old Boy Bravely Foils Robbery Attempt of 'Double SC' Gang Members." The article took up half the front page and described in vivid detail how Dylan had quickly and decisively locked one of the teens in his garage and had used the break-in tool against the other gang member, knocking him out cold.

His favourite part of the news story was the revelation that it was the carefully saved business card and paint can lid that ended up being definitive proof the Scarborough Scarers were responsible for both the vandalizing and all the break-ins.

His least favourite part of the article was the photo of him they included. It was his third-grade photo, taken on a very bad hair day.

Underneath his photo were two smaller photos

of the bad guys. They were head shots taken by the police, and showed both criminals from the side. On the photo of the thug who'd broken into his garage, three earrings were clearly visible. It was the guy buying peanut butter at Metro Dylan had suspected from the start. His name was Joe Drecker. The guy with the long, dirty hair who had stomped on the phone and slammed him into the wall was Brad Trottel. They were both repeating grade twelve at Hailey's school.

"Whoa!" Dylan grunted as Lucas landed on his lap with a thump after running across the room to leap on his older brother.

Dylan started tickling his younger brother. "Two broken wrists haven't slowed you down at all," he laughed. "Don't touch," he signed as Lucas began idly fiddling with the Velcro strap on the splint on his left wrist.

Instead of casts, Lucas was wearing two light-blue removeable splints to keep his wrists immobile while they healed. The splints were open on one side, secured with sturdy, Velcro straps. The splints were fast, easy to use, and could be taken off. They could be tightened or loosened to accommodate any increase or decrease in swelling. His mom was in charge of removing Lucas's splints for bath time and then putting them back on.

The x-rays of Lucas's wrists showed he didn't actually have broken wrists. He had two greenstick fractures. On Monday evening, Lucas had been jumping off the swing and had landed on the ground, both arms outstretched to brace his fall. His mother had explained that the force of his landing had caused one side of the bone to bend and the other side to break, in each wrist. It happened often in children whose bones were still soft and not fully hard, like an adult's.

Lucas abruptly jumped off Dylan's lap and headed in the direction of his room.

"You look tired," observed Hailey, coming into the living room, phone in hand, and plunking herself down on the couch.

"I am," agreed Dylan. It had been a busy, exhausting week for the Marcottes. On Monday, Dylan had been kept overnight for observation in the hospital as a precaution after his run-in with the thieves. On Tuesday before he was discharged from the hospital, the police officers who had responded to his 911 call stopped by his room with more questions for him. They had been very interested in seeing the business card and paint can lid Dylan had tucked away in his desk drawer the previous Friday.

When Dylan returned to school on Wednesday, he found himself the center of attention. Everyone wanted to hear him tell the story of how he had caught the notorious Scarborough bandits. He was sure, between relaying his adventure to his friends, teachers, neighbours, classmates, the police, and his family, he must have told the story dozens of times in the past four days.

"Ethan and his mom are coming up the walkway," said Dylan's mom as she set down tea cups and a pot of tea on their coffee table in front of the couch.

Dylan got out of his comfy chair to greet his best friend.

"I missed you yesterday."

Ethan took off his jacket and hung it in the closet. "Yeah, I think that's the first sleepover we've missed, like, ever. It's great your parents are letting me and my mom come over, even though you're still grounded."

Dylan nodded. "But in two more days my grounding's over."

During the questioning by the police, everything had come out about their illicit detective work at the park and the 'borrowing' of Hailey's phone. Dylan had been kind of glad to be surrounded by police officers when he shamefacedly admitted to his parents where and how he'd gotten the evidence the officers wanted to use. His mother's face had gone completely white and then her eyes had started to flash in that dangerous, 'you are in *so* much trouble' way he normally only saw her use on Hailey. His dad had taken off his glasses and was polishing them so vigorously it looked like he might polish a hole right through the lenses. He had also been running a hand through his short, dark hair, so much so, that all his hair was standing straight up.

"How much do you hate being stuck in your house, no TV, no phone, for a whole week?" asked Ethan.

Dylan shrugged. It hadn't actually been that bad. It was the scathing lecture he'd gotten before being grounded that was worse. He didn't think he'd ever forget their words that Tuesday evening.

"You went to the park even though we had strictly *forbidden* it. You put your friend in danger by being in an environment where he might have had contact with nuts. You took your sister's phone without permission and *lied* to her when she asked you where it was. It was not for you to try and catch a criminal! You're not to *ever* put yourself in danger like that again! For *any* reason! You scared the *life* out of us!"

Being grounded for a week meant he was confined to the house with both his parents home. And that meant there'd been a lot of time for him to finally speak with them about his worries. He'd been so relieved when his parents told him very emphatically they would *not* be adopting any more children. They stressed that Hailey, Dylan, and Lucas made them the perfect family.

"Even when we get in trouble and do things we're not supposed to and make you worry?" he'd hesitantly asked.

"*Especially* then," his mother had replied. "That's when you need us the most."

Both his parents had pulled him in for long embrace at his confession he sometimes felt left out of the family and forgotten.

"We're sorry you felt that way," apologized his mom. "Adopting you, Hailey, and Lucas, was the best decision your dad and I have ever made. We could never, *ever* forget about you."

Alexandra had paused a moment as she blinked away tears. "Maureen, one of the nurses who works on my floor, also has three children and she was telling me how every week, she devotes half a day just to spend time with one of her kids, one-on-one."

Alexandra had smiled at David. "What do you think, hon, about starting that tradition in our house?"

"That sounds fantastic," David agreed. "I'll make up a schedule we can review at this week's family meeting."

"Okay, let's get started," announced Dylan's dad, when they gathered for the Friday night family meeting, interrupting Dylan's thoughts about the past week.

"A lot has happened this week and we wanted a chance to go over it together, because everyone here has played a major part in the events," began Dylan's mother. She turned to Ethan's mom. "First of all, Nicole, we want to say how grateful we are to have you and Ethan as neighbours and to thank you for guiding the firefighters and police to our backyard so quickly and calmly on Monday."

Ethan's mom turned red. "No need for thanks, anybody would have done the same."

Dylan interjected, asking, "But how did the firefighters and police know where to come? That guy smashed the phone before I could give them my address."

"You called from our landline," explained Alexandra. "Our address would have shown up automatically on their computer. 911 dispatchers are obligated to send out an emergency response even when no one speaks into the phone."

"When you call 911 from a cell phone, though, Dylan," added David, "you *do* have to give an address, because all that shows up on the computer system is a telephone number, which is much harder to track down."

Dylan nodded. "That makes sense." He turned to Ethan's mom. "Sorry for interrupting. I've just been wondering how everyone knew where to come so fast."

Ethan's mom smiled over at Dylan. "No worries. I'm glad Ethan and I were in the right place at the right time. We were talking on the front steps about his day and he had just decided to go over and apologize, when he heard your bird call and took off to your place."

Dylan's dad cleared his throat. "Ethan, without your help that night things would have turned out very differently and we want to let you know how grateful we are to have you in our lives as Dylan's best friend."

Ethan blushed, and shrugged. "I didn't really do anything. I was coming over to say sorry after our fight and I just distracted the guy, that's all."

"Yeah, and when he was turned around, looking at you, that's when I had the chance to bop him over the head with that thing he used to break the lock," responded Dylan quickly.

"That *thing* is called a bolt cutter, Squirt," Hailey informed Dylan smugly.

Dylan took a deep breath. "Could you not call me names like Squirt, and Pickle, and Thing One anymore? It makes me feel small and kind of dumb."

Hailey flushed and fiddled self-consciously with her earring before speaking. "Sorry, Dyl, I'll try to stop, but calling you nicknames is gonna be a hard habit to break."

"That's okay," replied Dylan, just as his mother said, "I'm guessing you've not been appreciating Dad and I calling you nicknames, either."

Dylan settled back in his chair with a grin. Asking Hailey and his parents to stop calling him nicknames had gone perfectly. He'd directed his comment at Hailey with the secret hope his parents would feel addressed as well and it had worked! He glanced at his parents and at Hailey. Neither his parents nor Hailey seemed to be the least bit upset or bothered by his request.

"To change topics a bit," began his mother. "Your dad and I have been noticing whenever you get a compliment, Dylan, you tend to shrug it off and not accept it. You're so much more capable and smart than you give yourself credit for," she emphasized.

"Yeah," chimed in Ethan. "You're better at math than you think. You totally aced that math test the second time around. You just needed a bit more time to study. You were the one who came up with our cool alphabet-number code, and you were quick to learn the Morse code, even though you thought you wouldn't be able to."

"Speaking of being good at codes," added Dylan's dad. "Who was the one who helped me learn sign language when we were taking classes in the spring?" he said with a meaningful look at Dylan.

"Me," answered Dylan softly, staring down at the carpet. He had been worrying about not getting enough attention and here he was, the center of it, and it was making him feel uncomfortable. Uncomfortable, but good.

"Might as well get on this train, too," said Hailey, smiling over at her brother. "How many times have you got Lucas calmed down, because you knew what he wanted? You're observant," she continued. "You notice things we don't. That's what makes you so good with Lucas. And let's not forget you found his blanket that day, too."

Hearing his family and friends praise him and point out how smart and observant he was, made Dylan sit up straighter in his chair. Maybe he wasn't so dumb after all! And he had to agree, he did have a tendency to notice things other people missed.

"Okay, okay, I'm smart," laughed Dylan waving his arms in surrender. "But aren't you forgetting that big mistake I made?" He looked over at Ethan's mom. "When I thought I heard you saying the bad guy was caught?"

Ethan's mom laughed. "Number one, you shouldn't have been eavesdropping in the first place, and number two, wasn't it because of what you *thought* you heard that you and Ethan got into your first real fight?"

"Yeah," admitted Dylan grudgingly. "It's all my fault Ethan and I had a fight." He looked at everyone. "So I'm not as great as you're all trying to tell me!" he joked.

After everyone's laughter had died down, Dylan spoke again. "You know, I'm old enough you don't have to keep secrets from me, like about the bad guys breaking into cars and stealing stuff."

Dylan's parents nodded. "True, we sometimes

Two weeks later, on Halloween…

Dylan swung his empty, reflective, bright orange treat bag around as he and his family headed out to trick or treat.

"Wait!" he said, stopping suddenly.

"What's so urgent?" asked Hailey from under the sheet she had hastily thrown on for a ghost costume. She almost hadn't come along, thinking she was way too old to do something as juvenile as go trick-or-treating, but hearing that most of her friends were going out, *and* that Mrs. Fitz was supposedly giving out regular-sized chocolate bars, had made her change her mind at the last minute.

Dylan fished around in his coat pocket for his walkie-talkie. The police officers had taken up a collection to purchase Dylan and Ethan the radios after hearing the reason Dylan had taken Hailey's phone. The walkies had been delivered by two police officers a week after Dylan had trapped the thief in his garage. The police officers had included a card with the two-way radios that said Dylan would make an excellent police detective one day and they could hardly wait for him to join them on the force.

"Come in, Ethan, come in. We are set, ready, and costumed for trick-or-treating," he intoned seriously into the radio.

"Roger that," came the crackly voice of Ethan

through the radio. "Exiting the house now with my female parental unit."

Hailey snorted. "You two are insane."

Dylan grinned up at her and took her hand. He and Hailey had had a good chat after the family meeting with Ethan and his mom. She admitted that seeing him knocked flat on the ground and in danger that Monday night had made her realize how much she missed spending time with him. She had promised to "spend so much time with you, you'll get sick of me." Over the last two weeks, she'd kept her promise, even cancelling going over to Samantha's in favour of hanging out with him. She squeezed his hand back three times in the code she'd made up with him. One squeeze for every word of 'I love you'.

Ethan burst out of the house in his costume. "Ta da!' he said proudly. Ethan had wanted to make his costume this year, and the boys had worked on it for the last two weeks. He was wearing a large cardboard box from the grocery store, decorated to look exactly like a calculator. He even had a tin foil hat as the solar charging panel.

"You look totally authentic as a calculator!" said Dylan's dad.

"Yeah, and I can wear my coat underneath it and stay warm, so Mom doesn't worry," replied Ethan. "My EpiPen's in here too."

"Not that it isn't nice to have you along, David,

but aren't you staying in to give out treats and work on your novel?" said Ethan's mom, coming down the steps.

"Not tonight. I called my publisher to ask for an extension on finishing the book," replied Dylan's dad with a smile.

"Are you still with that little publishing company way out in Brantford?" asked Ethan's mom.

"I wouldn't be so quick to call them little," answered Dylan's dad. "They've taken on several talented authors over the last year and they're expanding rapidly. I spoke with the new CEO last week and she didn't have a problem with my request to extend the release date of the novel."

"You're lucky to have found such a great publisher to work with. If I ever decide I want to write a book about the life of a single mom, I'll give them a call first," laughed Ethan's mother.

"We should get going," said Alexandra, laughing as Lucas tugged insistently on her hand while signing, "Go now" repeatedly. "We have treats to collect."

"I love Lucas' costume," said Ethan's mom as the families set off along the sidewalk. "It looks warm and cozy."

Dylan's mom had found a soft, blue, warm material to make Lucas' Thomas the Train costume with. "Those Thomas costumes in the stores are way too thin and flimsy, so I thought I'd throw something together for Lucas that he'll wear *and* that fits around his splints."

"When do they come off?" asked Ethan's mom.

"Four more weeks, and they can't go by soon enough," answered Dylan's dad with a chuckle.

"Your costume turned out great," said Ethan as they walked up the path to the first house. "You totally look like Sherlock Holmes, famous British detective."

"Mom made it," replied Dylan as he adjusted the beige, green, and red deerstalker hat that had come to be closely associated with how detectives were often portrayed. "We spent all afternoon on it, just Mom and me. Dad took Hailey and Lucas to the park so we could work on it without getting interrupted." A warm feeling of contentment swept over him as he thought about their new family tradition of each child in the Marcotte family getting to spend quality time every third week with either David or Alexandra.

"Well, your costume looks authentic, which is more than I can say for Hailey's," observed Ethan. "It looks like she just grabbed an old sheet out of the closet and hacked two eyes out of it!"

"Yup," answered Dylan with a 'what are you gonna do about weird sisters' shrug.

As they trick-or-treated through their neighbourhood, Dylan couldn't stop smiling. It was the best Halloween ever. At every house they went to, people tossed extra candies into their bags, saying, "best homemade costumes I've seen tonight."

It was so much fun having his dad along. As he watched his dad pretend to swipe candies out of Lucas's bag and put them in his own pocket, he thought about what he had said after getting off the phone with his publisher last week.

"Your mother and I have been neglecting you and we're sorry we haven't paid more attention to you. That's going to change, effective immediately." He had pointed to the new 'quality time' schedule posted on the fridge, saying, "Dylan, tomorrow you and Mom have the afternoon together to do whatever you want." He gave his middle child a broad grin and a wink. "Our priorities became mixed up, especially mine. Family always comes first. *Always.*" he had repeated, before gathering Dylan up in a monster hug.

"Dylan! You just gonna stand there, daydreaming? Come on! Mrs. Fitz's house is next," said Ethan as he gently pushed his best friend along the sidewalk.

"Race you!" shouted Dylan, as he charged off down the sidewalk. It was the best time ever to be a nine-year-old in the Marcotte family.

DYLAN AND ETHAN'S ALPHABET
NUMBER CODE

A	1
B	2
C	3
D	4
E	5
F	6
G	7
H	8
I	9
J	10
K	11
L	12
M	13
N	14
O	15
P	16
Q	17
R	18
S	19
T	20
U	21
V	22
W	23
X	24
Y	25
Z	26

YES   25   NO   14   MAYBE   13

International Morse Code

1. The length of a dot is one unit.
2. A dash is three units.
3. The space between parts of the same letter is one unit.
4. The space between letters is three units.
5. The space between words is seven units.

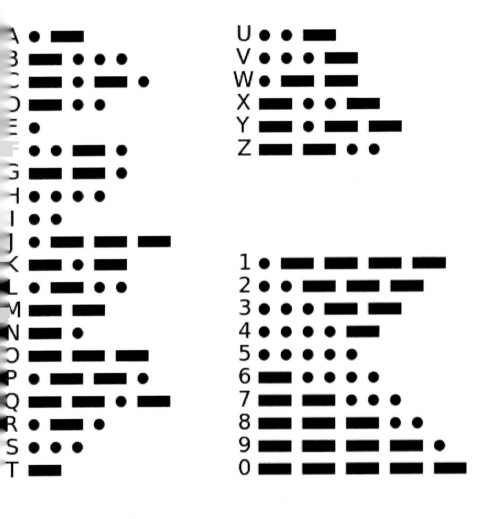

Sources

Chart of the Morse Code letters and numbers:
       en.wikipedia.org/wiki/Morse
code#/media/File:International Morse Code.svg
         authors: Rhey T. Snodgrass and Victor F. Camp 1922
         Image: Intcode.png and Image: International Morse
Code.PNG
accessed January 02, 2017

Cochlear Implants:
www.cochlear.com/wps/wcm/connect/au/home/understanding/he
aring-and-hl/hl-treatments/cochlear-implants
         accessed October, 2016

Explaining epilepsy to children:
       Kids Health
       kidshealth.org/en/kids/epilepsy.html#
       reviewed by Rupal Christine Gupta, MD, June 2016

       Epilepsy Clinic
       www.irishhealth.com/epilepsy/explain/.html
both sites accessed November 20, 2016

What happens during a seizure:
       Epilepsy Foundation – Warning signs of seizures
www.epilepsy.com/get-help/managing-your-
epilepsy/understanding-seizures-and-mergencies/warning-signs-
seizures

www.epilepsy.com/learn/epilepsy-101/what-happens-during-
seizure
  both sites authored by Steven. C. Schachter, MD, Patricia O.
Shafer, RN, MN, Joseph I. Sirven, MD
  both sites accessed November 20, 2016

EpiPens and Anaphylaxis:
  EpiPen Adrenaline Autoinjector – Youtube
  www.youtube.com/watch?v=pgvnt8YA7rs

How to use an EpiPen:
   (epinephrine injection, USP) Autoinjector
   www.epipen.com/about-epipen/how-to-use-epipen
   www.epipen.com/about-epipen/what-is-epinephrine

Women's and Children's Health Network
   Kids Health
Anaphylaxis – when an allergy can be really dangerous
   www.cyh.com/HealthTopics/HealthTopicDetailsKids.aspx
     above sites accessed October 27, 2016

Greenstick Fractures and Splints:
   Greenstick fractures
   en.wikipedia.org/wiki/Greenstick fracture

   Splints
     source.wustl.edu/2013/06/splints-favored-for-kids-forearm-
buckle-fractures
     authored by Elizabethe Holland Durando, June 11, 2013
   above sites accessed December, 2016